# The Painting

A fusion of good and evil, blended with science and religion, deep and thought-provoking

# Steven R Taplin

# Characters

Dexter Manning

Stan Thorne

Lyn Thorne

Melissa Thorne

Reuben Thorne

Raymond Shaw, parapsychologist

Enoch Raphael, The man from Rome

Detective Inspector Tim Farley

Inspector Paula Shelby

William 'The Kid' Bonné

Jasper the dog

Intentionally blank

# The First Letter of Dexter Manning

*To Inspector Farley of Hamden Police*

I, Dexter Manning, forward this brief memoir for your attention· Please, by all means, pass this on – it shall set the scene for the forthcoming events, thus, your investigations shall not be in vein·

I am an old man now· The life is fading from within this ageing soul, conceding to the inevitable· But I do not fear – There is another place, after all·

Now, please be so kind as to allow me to set a mental image – a picture in your mind, if you will· I'd like you to visualise my musty old living room; furnished in ancient oak, worn and stained from years of tobacco use, yet homely, nonetheless· My Grandfather passed on his tall, majestic clock and that same old clock still ticks away in the corner to this very day. Tick tock like the Grandfather clock. Well, at least it did when I wrote this. As you read, listen to the clock's rhythm – it's never out of beat, never out of tune. It has never let me down. My faithful ticking friend; sitting in the corner of my musty oak living room. Now, this may seem rather daft, but I named the old clock, after my Grandfather – Bertie. I was young when he died, so I have no memory of him. Bertie – that is my grandfather, not the clock, survived the trenches in 1917, only to die in the Blitz of September 1940. It was Friday 13th – very unlucky for him. He was in London that day. The bombs hit Buckingham Palace and the brand new Ford factory where he was visiting. I was just two years old at the time.

My father followed in his father's footsteps – a factory job at the Ford lines before going to war. They were both Great War heroes – the sort you just can't believe really existed. But they did exist and they were both mighty well decorated, too. I remember my mother telling me how my grandmother had tried to persuade us all to join her in Devon – to escape the Nazi bombs. She had already lost her husband and wasn't about to lose anyone else. My mother, my older sister and I moved, but my father could not be persuaded. My very first childhood memory is one that stung my mind for the whole of my life. I had only known my father for a short time and I remember the day when he announced that he was going to war. There was a far greater demand for soldiers than car production-line workers in 1943. I held onto my mother's hand one side and my sister's hand the other. We all looked him in the eyes as he spoke. 'I'll only be gone six weeks, two months tops,' he said. 'They just need a few more boys to help out with a job in Holland. I have to go through basic training first anyway – after which, they may not need me – the war should be over by Christmas they say. Just thought I'd better help out with the last of the war effort, you know.' I knew that my mother was crying – and I knew why. Yes, even a young boy can sense when something is wrong. That was the last time I saw my father; my only real memory of him. His leave

7

was cancelled three times, and when he was finally allowed to return to us, one of the big wigs in the war office, Monty, decided on finishing the war by Christmas. We'd all heard that statement before. In September 1944, my father dropped into Arnhem with the First Airborne Division. He never made it out. I have never been able to shake those memories of seeing my mother open a letter and collapse onto the kitchen floor in a flood of tears. I don't think she stopped crying for a month, maybe more. It was during the battle for Arnhem Bridge when my father became a war hero — he apparently took out an enemy gun emplacement that had just mown down thirteen soldiers. He saved his section of twelve men — at the cost of his own life. He saved twelve men, and left his family in ruin. He died on a Friday, too, and he was the thirteenth member of the section. I don't know what it is with Fridays and the number thirteen. Oh yes, I almost forgot. I was born on Friday thirteenth of May.

Following my Father's death, my Mother slipped downhill fast. By the time my sister and I were teenagers my mother had taken her own life. We grew up in Hamden, Devon, with my grandmother, Elizabeth, in the same old bungalow in Pines Avenue.

So, my grandfather and father were war heroes. Not me though – there was no war for me. I suppose there were one or two big conflicts of course – but none that conscripted young men from Hamden village.

My sister, Dorothy, found a loving husband and moved to Australia in the mad exodus of the sixties. A year later, my grandmother passed away and I was left alone to face the world.

Every day I have watched that old clock – old Bertie, to see whether any hint of life may arise – waiting and wishing for something from my past. I waited and waited, listening to the metronomic ticking. I waited for the day that my father and my mother would return to me. They never did.

Bertie the clock just ticked away, counting down the remaining seconds of my life. Tick. Tock. Like the Grandfather clock.

Let us return to the room. Let your eyes

drift along the ornate floral patterns. You will see several paintings hanging proudly. I often sat in my favourite rocking chair, slowly pitching forward and rolling back, forward and back, forward and back. The rocking motion is a great soothing feeling, don't you think? It was great to rock away and ponder life – or what was left of it. Now, if you would, please study the pictures upon the walls; a Van Gogh copy of Sunflowers brightening up one wall – visually at least – only hiding the deep hidden meaning of life and death that the Dutchman had portrayed. Another painting; a haunting picture of a frightened man; The Scream by Edvard Munch – an odd picture, to say the least, but one that I just couldn't do without. That was me in that picture. I studied it every morning – yep, it was me in there. Alongside this hangs, albeit, slightly askew, another painting. This one is another by Vincent Van Gogh; Starry Night. I would gaze into the darkness of the painting and allow myself to become absorbed inside the mystique. There was something alive within those paintings.

*And that gave me a wonderful idea.*

I removed my light-framed round spectacles and placed them neatly onto the wooden coffee table. With much effort I raised myself up from the rocking chair and made my way towards the old cupboard. Within those last days, it was always with great accomplishment whenever I moved around. My body weak and my mind slowly succumbing to the inevitable.

I opened the cupboard door and rummaged around on the middle shelf. They were still there – unopened paints, brushes and canvas. It was to be a hobby of which I would delight in sharing with the world. I wanted to show off an artistic flare. But that was then. Two years ago I had worked up some enthusiasm and some optimism. A past-time to fit in neatly with my weekly schedule of one visit to the supermarket and one visit to the bank – for my pittance of a pension. These would be the only times when I would actually make contact with the outside civilized world. Civilized – a word that had me cringe at the very thought of it; what was so civilized about modern society with all the greed and selfishness and anger and hatred· Oh yes, how I hated them all·

So, I had decided to paint· I had decided to put up one last picture· It would fit neatly between the Van Gogh paintings· And it would be my own work· Maybe it would be the very last thing I did in life· I thought about that briefly· There was no may be about it· This would definitely be the last thing I did·

I wheeled over a low nesting table which had long lost its partner· It was of similar oak to the bookshelf and table and had neat little wheels that made it a great piece of furniture· I rested the paints, canvas and brushes onto the table and slowly went out into the kitchen for a pot of water· Whilst there, I decided to pour myself a tall glass of Scotch with no ice· I never understood why people would water down such fine beverage with shavings of icebergs·

Back in the living room I sat back into the rocking chair and placed the canvas upon my lap· It was a box-canvas of about thirty inches by eighteen; quite a nice size· I opened a new brush and went to pick up the water paints but changed my mind· It had to be oil· An oil painting would be better; more life-like· So oil it was·

I had not planned out the picture nor filled my mind with visions of its image· I had not thought about the painting's structure or anything about its form· Somehow, I knew that it would be the brush that led the way, not the conscious mind·

The painting began to take place and as the brush worked its way around the canvas, I was beginning to smile for the first time in years· In front of me the image grew like a new child grows into the world· I had never been a father but had seen life grow all around me· The painting was a new life· It had become alive with the joy and eagerness of growing up and the expectations of its future· The greens and browns of the landscaped foreground complemented the rich colours of the stormy sky· A church was being built, stroke by stroke, its tower standing proud· Two gargoyles scowl from the roof; grotesque monsters with evil eyes, watching and waiting.

I sipped the scotch and replaced the glass tumbler back down onto the nesting table. I spoke to myself, finally. 'Looking good old boy, looking good.'

The picture had come along remarkably well and I was mighty pleased. The off-centred church was not one I recognised at first but I then thought hard and assumed it to be the old church over in Hamden Heath - where my parents were laid to rest. Oh yes, my father was brought back from Arnhem, albeit, many weeks later.

So, that was it - that was the church - Hamden Heath Medieval Church. The stormy grey sky with streaks of deep green shades and reddish backlight, the sunlight desperately seeking a way through the moody sky. A pathway, rough and uneven leads the eye from the foreground all the way to the church. To the left stands a lonely tree, bare of all its leaves; solemnly waiting for new life.

The painting was done. A work of art. I am happy; I had achieved something and could now enter the world of passing; enter my own new world within my own imagination. A new realm. Now, I could meet my family, and do whatever I liked.

So, it is with the utmost sadness that I must inform you of my departure from this world. Inspector, I have been set free and released into a new world. Do not despair for I am happy now. Am I in heaven? I do not know. I am somewhere far away. A place where pain and joy is one and the same. Is this the place that allows for all the beauty, debauchery and pleasures of one's desires? We can but only imagine.

This is my dominion. Tick. Tock.

Goodbye my dear friends, goodbye for now.

# Chapter Two

## A new investigation

It was the desk sergeant who gave Detective Inspector Tim Farley the news. She knocked on his glass office door and didn't wait for a reply.

Farley looked up at the sergeant. 'Yes?'

'Sir, there's a letter for you.'

'Who's it from?'

'I haven't opened it but it must have been hand posted – there's no stamp. It's addressed to you.'

Farley stood up and stretched, yawned and took the envelope. 'Thank you Sergeant.'

Inspector Farley was looking forward to his early retirement. A good part of his life had been served within the constabulary and although he would miss it, he wasn't going to regret leaving.

A short time later Inspector Farley made his way back round to the front desk where he found the young sergeant helping a member of the public with a simple enquiry. He waited briefly for her to finish.

'Sergeant, a word?'

'Yes Sir, what is it?'

'You said you thought that this letter had been hand delivered?'

'Yes that's right, sir.'

Farley frowned and then raised his eyebrows showing the age lines in his forehead. 'You know that the station doesn't have a letter box these days, don't you?'

The sergeant nodded. 'It was on this desk when I

arrived this morning. The night duty sergeant didn't see it being put there, maybe someone left it on the desk last night.'

Farley nodded. It was unusual for a member of the public to simply leave such an important message without speaking to anyone. Unless, he thought, that was the whole idea.

'The letter, message, is directed at me, personally,' he said. 'Yet I don't know this man.' He pointed with his left index finger at the envelope. 'Whoever this man is, or rather, was, has informed me of his death.'

The sergeant looked blankly at him, lost for words. She pulled a contorted expression with her mouth and then asked 'Will you investigate?'

'Damn right I will,' he replied firmly. 'I have to take this sort of thing very seriously.'

Inspector Farley returned to his small glass cube of an office and made a call. He collected his jacket, picked up his mobile phone and made his way out into the main operations room and over to another office which was much larger than his.

The police station interior had been refurbished recently and it now reminded Farley of a telephone call centre. Most of the main office was open plan and there were two small glass cubes set off to the sides. On one side stood Farley's cramped glass cube and to the opposite side of the room was the larger glass office. He didn't like the new office build at all – they gave no privacy.

He knocked on the glass door and made eye contact with both occupants. The sergeant inside nodded and then stood up. Farley entered the room.

'Can I have a minute?'

Sergeant William 'The Kid' Bonné was a fresh-faced

officer who had recently joined the firearms unit and his name seemed to live up to all expectations. He was a real hot shot in training and came top of the class. His French name was spelt differently to his namesake Wild West outlaw yet so close that his nickname could be none other than 'The Kid.' He would enjoy playing 'the kid' by talking the talk, in a somewhat poor wild-west accent.

In the office with Billy sat Inspector Paula Shelby; a veteran copper who had served many years on the beat. She was both well liked and admired within the station.

'Billy, I wasn't expecting to see you in here,' Farley stated. 'Not your usual hang-out.'

'No Sir, just had to clear up some fine dandy paperwork with the lovely Sergeant Shelby, I'll be on ma lonesome way.'

Farley grimaced, shook his head and then smiled, holding open the door. Billy thanked the inspector and made his way back out towards the armed section.

'That Billy is a funny character hey. What does he do around here anyway?'

'Normal stuff, the beat, paperwork, more paperwork, usual stuff. He gets bored but his time will come.'

'Well, I think he has a thing for you.'

'I have no idea what you are talking about, Inspector,' she replied, with a twisted, partly embarrassed smile.

'Oh come on,' said Farley. 'Any excuse and he's in here.'

'I'm old enough to be his mother, for goodness sake. I'm certainly not encouraging him, if that's what you think!'

Farley chuckled quietly and pulled up a chair.

'What can I do for you, Tim?'

'Paula, do you know anything about this?'

He handed her the envelope and she read the letter inside. Farley noticed how her eyes watered. He was sure there was a tear or two there. That was something he'd never seen from the strong woman. Paula was a strong character; she could handle herself and most men would soon learn that messing with her was not a wise thing to do. She handed it back and said 'No I've not seen this before.'

'It was left on the front desk last night. I'm going to take it seriously and I think you should come along.'

Shelby nodded. 'All right, you're the boss, I'll get my things.'

As they left the station she asked 'Do we need to have the uniform boys with us for this?'

'I've already arranged for a patrol car to join us at the address.'

The two inspectors drove out to the address; which had been written on the back of the envelope.

'I think I know the cottage,' Shelby said. 'Ivy Cottage is the little bungalow off-set from Pines Avenue isn't it?'

The in-car navigation system was already way ahead of her. It was highlighting the route clearly. Farley swung the unmarked Toyota into Pines Avenue and slowly pulled up behind a marked patrol car. The two uniformed officers stepped out of the police car in front and donned their flat caps.

Ivy Cottage was indeed set back from the quiet road and almost hidden between overgrown bushes, conifers and an enormous ancient ivy which seemed to swallow the building greedily. The neighbouring buildings were also bungalows and didn't overlook each other. Farley thought it looked quite idyllic in its own way – quiet, secluded, no through road with racing traffic. Nice.

A curtain twitched next door and a face appeared. An

elderly woman scowled at the four police officers and quickly withdrew from view. Farley thought this to be pretty normal; so often would neighbours inquisitively watch the police, yet fail to ask anyone what was going on. He couldn't understand that. Farley always had to know what was happening; even as a boy growing up in the busy city. Farley was always intrigued by police activity. Maybe that was why he became a policeman, he thought. Any accident, disturbance, missing person – he had to nose around and work out what went down. It was in his blood.

The uniformed boys went ahead down the overgrown pathway and knocked on the door.

No reply.

Knocked again.

Still no reply.

Shelby stepped over an old urn that was overgrown with weeds, and peered through the living room window. The curtains were open. The net curtains were hanging untidily allowing for gaping spaces for which to peer through.

'Can't see anyone inside here, Tim.'

Farley joined Paula and together they gazed through the window. Inside they could see a typical old living room with well-worn furniture and several pictures hanging from the wall. A tall-backed rocking chair faced away from the window, turned towards the centre of the room.

'Whoever it is certainly likes Van Gogh,' Paula remarked.

'Can I help you officers?' came a voice from behind.

The four police officers spun round to see an elderly couple standing at the edge of the pathway.

Farley spoke. 'Do you know who lives here?'

'Yes of course – we live over there,' the elderly lady

pointed to another bungalow the other side of the street. A well-kept place, neat lawns, tidy driveway, clean windows. 'Mr Manning lives here,' she said. 'Never see him though – keeps himself to himself.'

'Dexter Manning?' asked Farley.

'Yes that's right, anything wrong?'

'When was the last time you saw him?'

The elderly lady looked at her husband with a kind of guilty contemplation. It was almost as if she were asking him for a way out from answering the question.

'I'm not sure, must have been last week.'

Farley moved up closer to the couple. 'Does anyone around here actually know Mr Manning?'

The two elderly folk looked sheepishly at one another and then back at Farley.

'Didn't think so,' he said regretfully.

Farley nodded towards the officers. The two uniformed men went around the back of the house with Inspector Shelby. They found no reply from knocking on the back door and they could see nobody inside. The rear garden was just as overgrown and unkempt as the front. Inside the kitchen Paula Shelby could see an open oven door, nothing in there that she could see. There was, though, a made sandwich resting on a plate dead centre on the kitchen table. She studied it for a few seconds. It didn't have mould at all – it looked quite fresh.

'Sir, we are going in,' she called out.

Farley rushed round to join them. 'All right, guys, do it.'

The two policemen took it in turns to kick at the door until it succumbed and flew open, bouncing back against the stop.

One of the uniformed officers radioed back to base. 'Unable to gain response – entering property Ivy

21

Cottage, over.'

'Upstairs,' Farley pointed. Shelby and one of the officers hastily made for the bare wooden staircase.

Farley gave one look at the stale sandwich and headed off into the living room. He pushed open the door and was confronted with a jumble of old furniture, paintings, and a musty smell. A tall grandfather clock stood dormant, hands motionless, the pendulum dead centre. It had stopped at 12:05. It was a déjà vu. He knew this living room – that letter from Dexter was all he needed. He turned his head towards the front window and sighed out. There was the rocking chair but it had stopped rocking quite some time ago. Farley had been in the force for thirty five years yet despite his experience, each time he found a crime scene or dead body, he had the same old feeling; the combined feeling of sadness and despair. For any reasonable human being there was nothing which could really prepare them enough. All right, after seeing dead bodies one generally got used to it, but that's not to say it wasn't disturbing.

'Guys, down here.'

Inspector Shelby and the two officers stood behind Farley and stared at the rocking chair. In the chair sat a man, peacefully. His eyes were closed, his skin pale and grey. Lying on its side on the old Persian rug was a glass tumbler. An empty bottle of cheap scotch stood upright nearby. An empty bottle of strong painkillers lay alongside.

Farley leant forward and felt the cold neck that had no pulse. No air could be felt from the nostrils. He shook his head. 'Let them know,' he said to the officers.

The officer got back onto the radio again. 'Sierra tango we have an IC 1 male approximate age in the eighties, may need CS crew although looks self-inflicted. Will require coroner unit, over.'

Inspector Farley looked upon the man without touching him. If a crime scene officer or coroner wanted to make some investigations the last thing Farley needed to do was to touch the man any more than necessary. He felt sadness wash over him. This man had died alone, presumably by his own hand. I wonder why, he thought. Was it the fact that he appeared lonely?

'Sir,' Inspector Shelby said. 'In the letter he had written something about moving on...may I see it again?'

Farley removed the letter from his pocket and handed it to Paula.

'We are actually of the assumption that this is Dexter Manning, I suppose?'

Farley nodded. 'Still, we need to have that confirmed by his doctor, I don't think it's worth approaching the neighbours,' he added with a wry grin.

'It hints that he wanted to *move on*,' she said. 'I take it there's no next of kin.'

'That's what I thought, hence it'll be the doctor who will be required to formally identify.'

Farley gazed up at the pictures on the walls. He spotted a landscape painted in oils which looked fresh. He moved over towards it. Something happened. As he approached he was certain it shifted slightly. He glanced around to the others who were looking the other way. He looked back at the picture and it was hanging askew. He was sure it was straight a few seconds ago. He looked around at the others and they were still looking the other way. No need to bother them, so he turned back and the picture was straight again.

'Did you see...' he paused.

'See what?' Shelby asked, turning to face the inspector.

'Nothing, just, nothing, don't worry.' He then looked back at Dexter. Farley froze, almost terrified. Dexter's eyes opened. Dark, grey, lifeless eyes.

'Jesus!'

'Now what?' Paula called out.

Farley glanced towards the kitchen where Paula and the two officers had just re-entered. Upon looking back at Dexter, he saw closed eyes. Dexter's eyes were closed again.

The four sat themselves around the formica-covered kitchen table whilst awaiting the coroner. The stale sandwich had been disposed of. It was mainly Farley's idea – it was a mark of respect as much as anything. When the crime scenes branch announced they wouldn't be joining *the party* he became tense and angry. It wasn't the fact that they were not coming to the scene that had bothered him. It was the flippant remark about it being a *party* that had his back up. Always respect the dead, he'd say. Always respect the dead.

# Chapter Three

## RIP

When the coroner turned up he was only in the living room for a brief moment before moving into the kitchen.

'Well,' the coroner said in a dull tone. 'I'd put time of death to be around midnight. He's been dead for less than half a day that's for sure.'

Farley nodded. 'Was it the pills and the drink?'

'Won't know for certain until autopsy but I'd say that was the cause of death, yes.'

Farley had been informed that there were no ambulances available to collect the body and therefore it was the coroner who would be responsible. 'Do you mind staying for the doctor to arrive – he's going to confirm ID.'

'Not at all,' said the coroner. 'I'll need to wait for the unit to arrive – or black van if you wish.'

It never seemed appropriate. Farley had always thought of zipping someone into a bag and placing them into a black van to be slightly demeaning. It seemed rather unflattering to end up that way.

They sat quietly with the occasional low level whisper, as if trying hard not to wake up Dexter Manning. It was a non-written rule; never raise your voice or speak ill of the dead when a dead body awaits collection in the adjacent room.

After nearly a slow twenty minutes there was a knock on the door. Farley made eye contact with one of the officers and nodded his head in the direction of the front doorway. 'Let the doctor in, won't you.'

The officer stood up and went to the door.

'Nobody here, Sir.'

'Don't be playing games constable, not now.'

'I'm not Sir, see for yourself.'

Farley moved hastily to the front door and looked outside. The young constable was right – nobody was there. But just as they were about to shut the door, a compact saloon parked up behind the coroners car.

'Well I'll be damned!' said Farley in almost disbelief. 'How strange.'

The doctor eased himself out of the car and came down the overgrown pathway. 'Doctor Lionel Baxter,' he said offering his hand.

Farley shook his hand, 'Detective Inspector Tim Farley, pleased to meet you. He's in here.'

The doctor followed the inspector into the living room.

'We'll need to open the curtains – it's too dark in here,' announced the doctor.

'But,' Farley found it difficult to speak. He stumbled through the words. 'B-but the curtains...who closed the curtains?'

The police officers shrugged their shoulders. Paula remained speechless and shook her head.

'Well, okay,' Farley said, as he opened the curtains.

'That's him all right,' said the doctor. 'Poor old Dexter. You know, he came to me about six months ago and I prescribed anti-depressants.' The doctor felt for pulse and preceded with the basic checks. 'I can confirm that this is Dexter Manning.'

'Doctor,' Paula Shelby stepped forward and handed the doctor a single sheet document which he signed.

The doctor was in no doubt. Manning had distinctive features; balding grey hair, little meat on his bones, plenty of worry lines. And his round thin rimmed specs were on the floor beside the chair. It was him all right.

'Thanks Doctor,' Shelby said. 'That confirms our initial identification findings.'

Inspector Farley piped up. 'Doctor – you said that you haven't seen him for six months?' The doctor nodded and Farley continued. 'It sounds like he was depressed or something, so, why didn't you come to visit him?'

'I wish life was that simple inspector, I really do. You see, we have to rely on the patient coming to us. Before you say it, yes it stinks.'

Farley nodded. It seemed as if nobody cared about Dexter Manning.

'May I ask,' said the doctor, 'who found his body?'

'Nobody.'

'What do you mean?' said the doctor with puzzlement. 'Who informed you of his death?'

'He did.' Farley looked over at Paula and nodded as he spoke; 'Show him the letter.'

Paula took the letter from her jacket pocket and handed it to the doctor.

Doctor Baxter began to read out loud. 'Dear Inspector Farley...' he paused. 'So you knew him?'

'No.'

The doctor stared at the inspector for a few seconds before averting his gaze back to the letter. He continued to read. 'It is with the utmost sadness that I must inform you of my departure from this world.'

The doctor held the letter firmly in both hands. The paper trembled slightly. He removed his eyes from the words and looked across at Paula who was standing next to Manning. He saw tears in her eyes and she spun around quickly. The doctor looked back at the letter and then handed it back to Farley. I'd better get back to the surgery, inspector.'

'Thank you, Doctor Baxter.'

When the doctor had left, Farley went into the kitchen. 'Come on Paula, let's go, it looks like the coroner's van has arrived now.'

Paula nodded but did not speak. As she turned back to leave, something touched her. It felt as if someone had gently held her hand. In a split second, her mind was awash with dreadful images, death, pain, suffering. She saw clear visions of her father, Latin writing, a priest, a young blonde girl with hollow black eyes. She saw a grave with her own name on it. There was a gun – it fired. Paula gasped as the pain ran through her head. For a moment she thought she had seen a police officer shoot her. It wasn't in this house, somewhere else. And she could see the young officer's face, clearly. There were several people. And there was....a painting.

'Paula?'

Tim threw an expression of intrigue. Paula was motionless, staring blankly into the wall.

'Paula, you okay?

'Hey, oh, sorry,' she mumbled. 'I'm fine.'

Paula glanced down at Manning, ambivalently. He was not holding her hand, nobody was. She felt sadness, anger, confusion, yet there was an element of respect. She followed Farley out of the living room.

'Can I leave you two boys to clean up?'

The two uniformed policemen looked at one another and reluctantly agreed to stay and finish off in the house.

'Hey.' One of the uniform boys handed over another letter. It was wax-sealed in the old-fashion way. 'I found this on the windowsill.'

Farley took the letter, hesitated for a moment, then sliced it open with a knife. 'It's his will.'

'Shouldn't this go to a solicitor?' Paula asked, giving Farley a tearful look of reservation.

'It's addressed to me,' he replied, nervously. 'Why me?'

Paula shrugged her shoulders and half-nodded towards the will.

'He says very little apart from the paintings – he wants them auctioned at the charity shop.'

'Yeah, they do drop-in auctions – sort of casual bidding.'

'All right, I shall see to it.'

Farley took one final look at Dexter and then looked up at the mystical oil painting. Had it moved again? There seemed to be something about it; it had a kind of mesmerizing draw to it, almost as if you were getting sucked deep into the gloomy sky.

As they stepped outside, a single chime echoed around them, followed by a gentle metronomic ticking, which then stopped abruptly. Paula and Tim exchanged curious expressions.

'You all right?' Farley asked Paula as they made their way past the overgrown weeds and past the two coroners who had just arrived.

Paula nodded and they got back into the unmarked Toyota. And then she burst into tears.

'Hey, hey, come on,' Farley let Paula rest her head on his shoulder. He'd never seen this in all of the fifteen years he'd known her.

Paula sniffed and wiped her eyes. 'I'm so sorry Sir, this is really unprofessional.'

'Not to worry,' he replied. 'You're only human. You know, you'll have me crying soon.'

She allowed a slight chuckle to escape the forlorn face and then pulled away from him and sat upright in the seat.

'We'd better go,' she sniffed again. 'Nosey neighbours. Look, curtain twitching again.'

Farley glanced out of the right hand side window and spotted the curtains twitching. It always annoyed him. Neighbourhood watch my ass.

'I wish they'd paid a bit more attention to poor Dexter. Maybe just done the shopping for him, even said hello would have helped.'

'Tim, don't beat yourself up over it.' Paula watched him as he started the car and began to drive away. 'Have I ever told you what happened to my father?'

Farley shook his head. 'No.'

She glanced sideways through the window and watched the urban scenery flash by. 'The same thing. My father died the same way when I was just a kid.' She bit her lip to prevent herself from crying. It may have been ancient history but the pain was still there. It always would be. 'He left us because he couldn't face the money shortage we had.' Paula let the tears roll down her face. Tim felt choked up inside.

'I'm sorry, Paula.'

'It's all right – it's just that letter seemed to bring it all back. All the sadness from all those years ago came flooding back. I saw.....something too, like a vision of death.'

'It was a terribly sad letter and we all felt something in there.' Farley looked across at her. 'You've never spoken about your family.'

'Not much to say about them really,' Paula verbally handed over the only details she knew. 'My father's name was Milton; he moved here from Australia, met my mother and then I was born. But my parents just fought and argued and then some, until finally they divorced. I grew up in the battleground of a feuding couple. I decided to live with mum. It is regrettable that we gave up on him. I never bothered to visit, and...'

Tim saw her tears and noticed her swallow hard. He

30

so needed to hold her hand, to hug her. Totally unprofessional he mused.

Paula smiled at the inspector; she saw him as a friend, not the chief. 'Sorry, Tim, where was I? Oh, yeah, my father died alone of liver failure. Ten years we hadn't even made contact with him. Ten years, Tim.'

'I'm sorry to have bothered you with this, Paula.'

'No, Tim, it's fine. Actually, I have really wanted to talk about my life with someone. You know, in the police force it's all macho and no emotion. I see the public break down in tears and I have to remain stone-faced. It's a difficult thing to do, Tim. All these years and I've listened to people's problems and watched people fall apart, and I've never had the chance to talk about my problems, my history, my family.' Paula allowed a wry grin to develop. 'A few years ago Mum and I looked into our family tree – a tree with half its branches missing. All I found out was that Granny Dot, sorry, that was a childhood name I gave her – her name was Dorothy. Anyway, she never gave out her maiden name. Mum knew it but never told me. I never asked I guessed. All I know is that Dorothy lived through the war and moved down-under. But this is weird; how can I put this, um, back in the house I looked at that big painting and could have sworn I saw a gravestone with the name Dorothy Manning. Weird hey? There's something odd about that painting. Does this make sense?'

'Yeah, it does actually. But I'd like to hear more about you, Paula. What do you say about a coffee at the Contour Coffee place before we head back to the station?'

Paula nodded. 'Yeah, I'd like that.'

Farley rolled the Toyota off the main road and into a large car park that served several large food outlets and

31

the coffee shop.

They sat themselves down and Tim raised his mug and clinked it against Paula's. 'Here's to Dexter Manning.'

'To Dexter, rest in peace.'

# Chapter Four

## A Charity Auction

## Sunday 8<sup>th</sup>

'Hey, Stanley, come and have a look at this painting.' Lyn Thorne gesticulated for her husband to come over. 'Take a look at this picture – it draws you into it.'

Forty three year old Stanley Thorne glanced over at his wife before looking at the picture. 'Do we really need another painting?'

'No, I just like it, that's all.'

Stan walked away and shifted sideways over to the two children. 'Found anything interesting?'

Melissa showed her father an oil painting of a horse splashing through shallow water.

'Not you as well' Stan groaned. 'What is it about you women and paintings?'

Lyn spoke up. 'Nothing to do with women, Stan. Can you think of any famous male artists?' She grinned at her husband. 'Melissa, what do you think of this one?'

Melissa looked across at the painting. 'Oh wow!' she exclaimed. 'That's amazing.' She replaced the horse painting and moved over to join her mother. 'Who painted this?'

'Look,' Lyn pointed at the bottom right. 'A man called Dexter.'

'Let's take it,' Melissa said, smiling.

Stan and Lyn had two children, Melissa and Reuben. Both had reached their teens long before they hit twelve. Growing up seemed to accelerate each year. Lyn had often commented just how quickly the twins had matured. Both were now sixteen, yet, despite their obvious independence, they still enjoyed a family outing to the charity shop once in a while.

'That's awesome!' exclaimed Reuben. 'Take it – we can hang it in the hallway.' He began to examine the work of art.

'All right,' Stan sighed. 'Let's put in a bid.'

The others continued to stare into the picture. 'Look at the way that path twists through the grave yard. It sort of leads you into the church,' observed Melissa.

'Creepy church,' Reuben remarked. 'Mum?'

Lyn hadn't moved.

'Mum?' Reuben nudged his mother. 'Come on, let's go and bid for it.'

Lyn jolted back into reality. For a moment, she thought that she was actually inside it. She felt herself walking along the eerie path, through the arched door and into the old church. She saw the rows of wooden pews, the altar, the stain-glass windows and a painting. She re-imagined the scene – the painting. It seemed to be displayed in a prominent position. And there was something strange about one of the stain-glass windows – it was just a face of an old man. 'There's something about this painting. Weird.'

The Thorne family made a reasonable bid for the painting and wandered casually back to the little café that was attached to the charity shop.

It wasn't a long wait. A man dressed in a smart black suit approached them. Apparently there were no other bids for the painting that day, so from then on it had become property of the Thorne family.

They wandered out of the shop and over to their six-year-old Honda compact. The painting, being one metre long and half a metre deep, barely made it into the car. The kids sat with it on their lap.

The journey home was just fifteen minutes. Stanley made an observation. 'You're very quiet, Lyn.'

Lyn's pale blue eyes continued to gaze through the windscreen and along the road ahead. Rain began to fall, gently, mini drops of water settled on the glass before being wiped away forever. 'Life is just like a drop of water.'

Stan glanced over briefly. 'What?'

'Life is just like a drop of water.'

'Yeah I heard you the first time, what I was asking... oh never mind.'

'Think about it, Stan. A rain drop grows inside a cloud...'

'Oh, here goes with the science,' Reuben muttered.

Lyn ignored him and continued. '– water vapour condenses around tiny particles of dust. The water grows, just as any life grows. It falls, picks up more water vapour and grows bigger. Then it falls, say, onto the windscreen and gets wiped away forever. It dies, right there and then, just like any life.'

'That's a bit deep, mum,' Melissa announced. 'You've been reading my science books again, haven't you?'

Lyn grinned.

'As long as that's all you've been reading. You'd better not have read my diary, mum.'

Reuben laughed. 'There's nothing in your diary that mum doesn't already know.'

'What?' Melissa yelled. 'You've been reading my diary, Reuben.'

'Only the juicy bits like the bit about Raymond – that geeky uni guy.'

'Mum,' Melissa shouted. 'Tell him not to go through

my stuff.'

'Don't go through her stuff, Reuben.'

'Oh, thanks mum, that's a great help. Why don't you tell him off?'

'Oh get with the program, Melissa. Everyone has read your diary.'

'What, bloody hell, that's personal stuff.'

'Mind your language, young lady.'

'Oh, real mature, Mum. You're telling me to mind my language after you sneak through my stuff and read my journal.'

'Mum,' Reuben whispered. 'Did you read the bit about...'

'Get lost Reuben,' Melissa hit her brother in the arm, hard.

'Oh, I'm in such pain,' Reuben announced, grinning. 'Oh, it hurts so much. Mum, she's beating me up.'

Melissa hit him again.

'She hit me again,' he said, trying to hide his laughter.

'Well hit her back,' Stan said.

'Thanks dad, at least you're on my side.'

'I'm not on any side. Fight all you like, just don't damage the painting.'

Then Reuben pulled a long strand of Melissa's golden hair.

'Oww-a. God, why did I have to have a twin brother that's such a jerk?'

'I'm telling mum that you called me a jerk!'

Lyn turned her head slightly. 'Mum doesn't care if Melissa called you a jerk.'

Reuben stuck out his tongue at Melissa.

'Grow up,' Melissa responded. 'Get a life, jerk.'

'Oooh! Ouch! Anyway, I've got more of a life than you, nerd-brain.'

'Will you two knock it off,' Stan yelled. 'Both of you – act your age.'

Lyn added, 'You kids couldn't wait to grow up – now I think you've grown down!'

'Grown down?' Melissa asked. 'What does that mean?'

'It means that you have become silly little children again, not growing up into mature adults.'

'Oh thanks,' Melissa said. 'You can talk, Mum.'

'Will you three stop bickering and give me some peace,' Stan grinned through his stern features.

Lyn pulled a comical face at her husband. She had always known that she had a perfect family – a loving husband who was gentle, calm and usually chilled out. In fact, she often thought that if he chilled out any more he'd be horizontal. And she had two great kids – blonde-haired twins with good looks and great personalities. Okay, they weren't always perfectly behaved kids, but then who is? The silliness and bickering was all part of growing up. Lyn knew it – she'd been there and done it – she'd been a teenager once.

'You know,' Stan said, 'They must get it from your side.'

Lyn gave a part-crooked smile.

'I mean,' Stan added, 'I'm too easy going – those two kids get all their rowdiness and argumentative side from you.'

'Thanks, darling. You're such a loving husband!'

Stan eased the car along Pines Avenue, past the row of old cottages and into the short cul-de-sac. 'I see that Ivy Cottage is up for sale. I heard that the old guy died not so long ago.'

Reuben lent forward. 'I heard that the old bloke died

37

of loneliness.'

'Shut up Reuben,' Melissa said. 'That's not very nice.'

'Why? I'm not being nasty – that's just what I heard.'

'People can't die of loneliness, can they?'

'I don't know,' Lyn replied. 'Whatever happened, we need to give him some respect.'

'Was he a nice guy?' Melissa added.

'Never met him.'

'Did anyone actually know him around here?' Reuben asked.

Stan shrugged his shoulders. 'Don't know.'

'Well, he's gone to a better place now,' Lyn announced.

'What does that mean?' Melissa said. 'I hate it when people say that. It's such a stupid comment. What better place? Come on.'

Reuben nudged his sister. 'Maybe he's gonna come back and haunt you, wooo, wooo!'

'Grow up.'

'I am grown up. In fact I'm slightly taller than you.'

Melissa shook her head. 'Whatever.'

The car rolled up onto the driveway and stopped short of the garage. Lyn stepped out and opened the rear left door and eased the painting out. Stan allowed the twins to exit the car and locked it, watched the lights flash and checked the door to confirm that it was locked securely. Not that there were any issues with car theft in the quiet road – it was just common sense.

Jasper, the family two-year-old Retriever barked excitedly when he heard the Honda. He was at the door, tail wagging, before Lyn had even opened it.

# Chapter Five

## Raymond

Stanley positioned the painting neatly on the wall. 'That looks good,' he said, closing one eye and lining up the frame against the nearby door. 'Lyn, could you mark the edges with that pencil,' he said, nodding his head towards a pencil that lay on the floor.

Lyn made some outline makings and Stan removed the picture. He carefully measured up the hanging points and drilled two holes, knocked plugs into them and screwed the screws in. He used the picture wire that was attached to the painting and hung it up.

'There, perfect.'

'Aren't you clever, dear,' Lyn declared amusingly.

'I'm good for some things!'

'Reuben, Melissa,' Lyn called. 'Come and see what you think.'

Both of the kids nodded in appreciation. It looked good. It worked well with the surrounding magnolia walls. The picture hung there as if it was *meant* to be there.

'Right,' Lyn said. 'What does everyone want for dinner?'

'Um...' Melissa hesitated. 'Mum, if it's all right with you...can I skip dinner?'

'Why?'

'She wants to meet this Raymond character, Mum.'

'Reuben let your sister speak for herself. Well?'

'It's just that, um, he um...'

'Melissa, for goodness sake – stop saying um, um,

um, all the time.'

'All right. Can I see Raymond tonight?'

'I knew it!' declared Reuben. 'Melissa's got a boyfriend, Melissa's got a…'

'Shut up,' Melissa smacked him on the back of his head.

'Stop it you two. Melissa– I'm going to let your Dad decide on this one.'

'Oh, Mum…'

'Don't *oh mum* me.'

'Dad?'

'I'm not sure we ought to let you date some guy we've never met,' Stanley said seriously. 'I don't even know anything about him.'

'I do,' Reuben interrupted. 'He's twenty three and goes to university and studies Parapsychology, he has a…'

'Reuben be quiet,' Stan shouted. 'Well, Melissa? Hang on – he studies what?'

'Dad, he's a really nice guy and…'

'Oh I bet he is,' Reuben said. 'Really nice.'

'Reuben go and help your mother in the kitchen. Now.'

Lyn threw her husband a displeasing look. 'If that's not a hint for me to cook dinner then I don't know what is. Come on boy, kitchen.'

'Oh, Mum.'

'Oh just do it, leave your sister alone for once.'

Melissa nodded a thank-you at her mother. She turned back to Stan. 'What about…um…what about inviting him here – for dinner?'

'It's a bit short notice, isn't it?'

'No not really. Anyway, he's only down here for a week – he goes back to university soon.'

'What, is he on a break?'

'Visiting his family – they live in Cedar Walk.'

'Oh, that's convenient,' Reuben called out. He popped his head round the kitchen door. 'One street over – only a minute walk – yeah, invite him over – can't wait to see if all the things are true!'

'What things?' Stan asked.

Lyn stopped her son answering with a hand over his mouth. She shook her head and whispered, 'No, leave it.'

Stan stood tall and proud. He held his chin as one does when in deep thought. 'All right. Give him a call.'

Melissa stretched up and gave her father a kiss on his cheek. 'Thanks, Dad.'

Stan grinned and shook his head slowly. *Teenagers*, he thought.


Dinner was almost ready when the doorbell rang. Jasper the Retriever rarely bothered to bark at the door. He saw it pointless. What was the point of barking at a door? It was all about who was on the *other side* of the door. And Jasper could always tell who it was. This time, he gave one soft bark – a sort of warning shot across the bow. A simple announcement – *I'm in here and I sense that you are a stranger – don't mess with me.*

The simple, old-fashioned chime of the bell reflected Stan and Lyn's attitude to modern life. They couldn't care for silly tones, or any other wacky entrance toys such as croaking frogs. A simple life, a simple house, tucked away in the corner of an average suburban cul-de-sac.

'I guess you must be Raymond,' Stan managed to beat Melissa to the door – who bounced up and down excitedly on her heels.

'Hello Sir, Raymond Shaw,' he said politely, offering

41

out his hand. 'Pleased to meet you.'

'Likewise, please, come in.' Stan smiled at the student and shook his hand. He had already begun to like him. He hadn't been called *Sir* since that unfortunate incident in the White Lion pub – when, after a few too many drinks, Stan had an encounter with a policeman. That was the last time he was called Sir. Stan remembered it well. *'Sir, you are making a scene. Would you kindly make your way home or you may face being arrested. Sir, I will not ask you again…'*

Melissa made eye-contact with Raymond, before averting her eyes to the floor, almost feeling slightly embarrassed, or awkward. This was, of course, the first time she had ever brought a boy home – not a boy, a man.

Lyn looked the handsome man up and down. He was quite slim, wore tiny round specs and had his dark brown hair gelled back in a wave. She shook Raymond's hand and then, to Melissa's delight, so too did Reuben.

'So what is it that you study?' Reuben asked.

'Oh Reuben,' Lyn nudged him. 'Let Raymond settle in before you bombard him with questions.'

'Oh, that's all right Mrs Thorne.' Raymond looked around the small kitchen. He noticed the pine-veneer, the fake oak laminate and the family portrait hanging askew on the wall. 'In answer to your question, I study parapsychology.'

'That's real kinda spooky!' Reuben remarked.

Raymond chuckled politely. He'd heard all the jokes and he'd heard so many people tell him that he was wasting a degree doing a pointless subject. He cared not – it was a boyhood interest and a subject he thoroughly enjoyed. He noticed that Lyn seemed slightly puzzled. 'Parapsychology is the study of anything paranormal –

you know, clairvoyance, psychokinesis, apparitions and so on.'

'So you believe in all that?' Stan asked openly.

Raymond took a second or two before answering, making it appear that he was working out the best and most logical answer. 'I can't say that I do or do not believe. I mean, yes, there must be some forms of paranormal activity – let's face it, there have been so many stories over the last five thousand years – there must be something in it.'

'A bit like the Bible,' Reuben said. He looked at the others who gave him questioning expressions. 'What? I just think that for two thousand years, and more, people have believed in certain events so strongly – that there might be something there. Maybe Jesus did exist, and maybe he really did perform miracles.'

Lyn gave her son a rewarding look. She was unfamiliar with this part of him. For once, Reuben was the philosopher, the 'thinking one,' instead of the cocky and daft one. 'Where did that come from?'

'What? I'm not all stupid, you know.'

'We know, dear. It's just great to hear you come up with such deep ideas.'

'Dad agrees, don't you?'

Stan raised his eyebrows and nodded.

'So,' Melissa changed the subject sharply. 'I hope you like chilli con carne – don't worry, it's not too spicy. I hope.'

'Ah ha!' Reuben grinned, devilishly. 'Don't forget that I made it!'

'You'd better not have...'

'Only kidding,' Reuben said. 'Would I do anything like put too much chilli in it?'

Melissa threw him a telling expression.

Raymond had taken well to the family. The conversation bounced back and forth, around the table, as they tucked into their chilli con carne. Both Stan and Lyn had grown an instant fondness for the student. He was mature, polite and well spoken. Although he did study an off-beat subject, still, they weren't to question his tastes in life or his choice of education. Stan himself had often mused over his own choice of subject at university. He had studied History and Religion – he'd never once needed it since graduation. The subject rarely cropped up in his current employment as a manager of a paper mill.

Then, Stan spotted the glass portrait of the family. He wasn't one for ever allowing a picture to hang crooked. 'I'm sorry, that picture isn't straight.'

'Oh, come on love,' Lyn said. 'Don't worry about it.' She began to clear the table. Raymond halted her.

'Please, Mrs Thorne, let Melissa and I clear up.'

Lyn hesitated momentarily. 'Oh, no, I couldn't let a guest do the dishes.'

'Nonsense. Please.'

'All right, okay with you, Melissa?'

Melissa nodded.

Stan moved over to the family portrait. It was a small picture of the four enjoying a sunny day on the canal. It was a one-off, spur-of-the-moment day out – they had rented a canal boat with its driver. The picture showed a happy family, lounging on a boat in the summer sun.

'Oh, Dad, you and your fussiness!' Melissa said.

He then paid a visit to the new painting in the hallway. He remembered that he had not wiped off a mark on the frame. But as he touched it he yelped. 'Ah! What the...'

'What is it?' Lyn asked.

Jasper sat bolt upright and barked.

'I've just burnt my fingers on the frame.'

'Oh, you couldn't have done,' replied Lyn.

'Well, come here and touch it.'

Melissa noticed how Raymond seemed rather interested, although silent, he was certainly concerned.

'There,' Lyn said, touching the frame. 'It's not hot.' She wiped off the mark for Stan.

'Well, look,' Stan held out his hand. There were no burn marks. 'Well they are damn painful.'

Later, having chatted for what seemed like hours, Raymond made a polite request to make his way home. As he walked out through the hallway he stopped.

'That's some painting you have here.' He studied the picture for a few seconds. 'It has some great brush strokes and wonderful colours – almost feels like you could actually walk into the scene.'

'We bought it today at a charity shop auction,' Lyn stated. 'You know, just a light auction where you go in and have a look at some junk, put a bid on, wait a while and see if you've bought it.'

'Junk you say? I certainly wouldn't call this work of art a piece of junk, Mrs Thorne.'

Just as he turned away, Raymond felt someone brush his hair. The others were not close enough to touch him. He glanced back into the painting and felt cold.

# Chapter Six

# The painting

## Monday

Monday morning saw a colourful sunrise. Reuben opened the curtains. The light burnt his eyes briefly, he yawned, turned and flopped back down onto his untidy bed.

'Reuben,' Lyn yelled up the stairs. 'Come on, you'll be late.'

The teenager groaned an unrecognisable grunt before dragging himself into the bathroom.

'Did you see the sunrise this morning?' Melissa asked. 'What's that saying when you see a red sky?'

Lyn continued to monitor the toast. She never trusted that old toaster – it seemed to have a mind of its own; turn your back on it for one minute and you have charcoal. 'That expression you are looking for – red sky at night, shepherds' delight, red sky in the morning – shepherds' warning.'

'Oh yeah, that's the one,' Melissa stated. 'Well anyway, the sky was really red this morning.'

'Well, let's hope it's not an omen.'

'It may be for the shepherds, hey?' Melissa said wittily.

'What's this about a red sky?' asked Stan, stretching as he entered the kitchen.

Lyn watched the toaster pop up. 'Melissa said that it was a very red sky this morning.'

'It's cloudy.'

Lyn hadn't actually looked outside. 'The weather man said that we are in for rain.'

Stan grabbed a slice of toast and felt the heat burn his fingers again. 'Damn it!'

'Those fingers still hurt?'

Stan sat himself down and looked up at Lyn. 'They still hurt like hell. That was so weird yesterday.'

Lyn put the other slices of toast on a plate and lowered them onto the table. 'Reuben, hurry up.'

'Mum,' Melissa sipped her coffee and continued. 'What did you think of Raymond?'

'Seems a very nice chap.'

'Would it be all right if I went to see him at university some time.'

Both Lyn and Stan answered simultaneously, with mouths full of toast. 'NO!'

Melissa looked deep into the mug of dark roast coffee. 'Thought you'd say that.'

'Then why did you ask?' replied Stan.

Just then Reuben sauntered in.

'About time,' Lyn said. 'Park your keister down and have some toast.'

'Amazing sunrise this morning wasn't it?'

Melissa looked up from her mug. 'You saw it too?'

'Couldn't miss it – really bright red and yellow – like an oil painting.'

Melissa glanced over at her mother. 'There, you see – I wasn't imagining it.'

'Never said you were.'

'Still, don't know what you kids had been smoking but believe me, it's been cloudy all night and it's still cloudy now.'

'Dad,' Melissa said, lowering her mug onto the table and frowning. 'Firstly, neither of us smoke, and secondly, we know what we saw.'

47

'All right,' Stan said, putting up his hands in a comical surrendering gesture. 'You win.'

'Anyway, Dad, how's the finger?' asked Reuben, dropping a piece of buttered toast on the floor for the dog.

'Reuben don't feed him toast.'

'He likes it.'

'Anyway, fingers – plural – I burnt two of them. And they are still sore.'

Melissa remembered something that Raymond had said before he left. 'Raymond reckons that the picture had been moved by someone before – and that's why you got burnt.'

'One of us may have knocked it but that doesn't explain why it was red hot.'

'He says that it was moved by a spirit – and that not all spirits are cold, some leave hot finger prints.'

Reuben laughed. 'Are you for real?' He chuckled again. 'And it sounds like your boyfriend has been on the spirits – like glug, glug, glug!'

'Reuben's right,' Stan said. 'A spirit – with hot fingers? Come on!'

'Believe what you like, Dad, but you burnt yourself and straight after that the frame was cold again. Explain that.'

Melissa had asked a question with no logical answer. None of them knew how it had happened.

'Oh, and Reuben – he's not my boyfriend – he's a friend, something you wouldn't know anything about.'

'Now, now, Melissa, stop that.' Lyn gave her a scowl.

'It's all right Mum,' Reuben said calmly. 'She won't succeed in winding me up – but I may just set the evil spirit on her!'

'Mum, tell him to stop – that's not funny. Reuben,

48

you should never tempt fate – never tease the devil.'

Reuben looked bemused. 'What?'

'It's something that Raymond said.'

Reuben repeated her words in a childish tone, '*It's something that Raymond said.*'

'All right you two; just take your arguing to school and get out,' Lyn motioned them out of the kitchen. 'Scram! Shoo!'

Lyn opened the blinds and sat down again with Stan. They both looked out of the window and up to the cloudy sky, in deep thought.

Half an hour later Stan kissed his wife goodbye and left for work. With Stan and the kids gone, Lyn was alone in the house. Not for the first time, by any means. She had seen them leave for school and work a thousand times. But this time it felt different. She had a terrifying feeling that she wouldn't see them come back.

Lyn told herself to snap out of it and tuned her thoughts into doing the chores. That was the housewife in her – always checking on the kids, checking on the husband, cleaning this and cleaning that. But, Lyn secretly enjoyed it – at least she didn't have to sit in the rat-run of rush-hour traffic and be bossed around by the big bad boss. Lyn grinned at her own thoughts; she had plenty of time to do whatever she wanted, within reason, of course. 'Jasper,' she called. 'Do you want to go for a walk?'

The bouncy Retriever leapt up and out of his basket where he had sat so patiently. His tail wagged fast, almost knocking over a vase of withering cut flowers. She frowned at the roses. There was something eerily odd about them – how had they become withered and crispy? They were fresh-cut yesterday. Lyn touched a petal. It crumbled like ash. Black, crumbly, ash.

'Weird.' She muttered, then glanced back at Jasper who had by now achieved her full and undivided attention. 'All right, all right, calm down Jasper. Let's go.'

For some unknown reason, Lyn had decided to take Jasper out the front door. As they passed the painting, Jasper began to pull back, whimpering softly.

'What is it Jasper? There's nobody here.'

But Jasper thought otherwise. Somebody definitely *was* there. He could see something in the wall. However hard Lyn tugged at his lead, Jasper would not move. Lyn released the lead and Jasper ran to the back door, barked, and wagged his tail.

'Oh, so it's all right to use the back door is it? Come on you silly sausage! Let's go for that walk.'

It was a peaceful and relaxing walk around the park and up to the large duck pond. Jasper spotted two Moorhens and ran towards them. The pair of birds flapped away in an ungainly fashion and settled further into the pond, away from the dog. Jasper ran around into the reeds, sniffed about for a while and then returned to Lyn.

'Go on, if you must,' Lyn said, showing him an old, chewed tennis ball. She threw the ball into the water and Jasper leapt in with a huge splash.

'Come on boy,' Lyn called. 'Come on.'

Jasper retrieved the ball and brought it back to Lyn. After six goes, Lyn became bored and told the Retriever that they must return home. Lyn popped his collar back on and he led her home. Jasper always led the way. It was the thing they had. Lyn would lead him out, Jasper would lead her back home. She loved him. She loved him as a family member. She often wondered how she would feel if something terrible would happen to him. Back inside the house, Lyn gave the dog a bath, dried him off, and told him to settle down in his big dog basket in the kitchen. She then remembered something.

'Damn,' she exclaimed. 'The gas meter reading.'

Lyn found a recent gas and electricity bill that was an estimate. She had decided to give them the actual readings so that they would not pay too much. That was a week ago. Still, better late than never. Lyn went outside, read the meters and re-entered through the front door. As she shut the door, something happened. Something touched her neck. She thought it was a spider and frantically slapped her neck, whipped off her loose top and checked. She hated spiders. But there was nothing there. She felt something again, this time it felt as if a feather was slowly working its way down her back. She turned fast. Nothing there. Lyn looked into the painting. She began walking up the churchyard path, gliding gracefully towards the old church. The two gargoyles growled irritably. She ignored them and entered the church. There, in front of her, at the altar, was a sacrifice. An ancient priest began to chant.

*'Sacrifico aeternam. Nam dominus meus.'*

Lyn began to feel the burn of teardrops on her cheeks. She stood, motionless, staring at the dog; a golden Retriever – a sacrifice to the devil.

The priest, dressed in long black robes, looked over at Lyn. His eyes were dark and hollow, his skin grey and wrinkled. A lock of grey hair fell untidily over his forehead.

*'Diabolus enim, accipe sacrificium.'*

'No!' Lyn screamed. The knife began to lower. 'No!'

51

# Chapter Seven

## Visions

Lyn closed her eyes. She felt warmth upon her skin. She felt moisture on her cheek. Her body was trembling with fear. She heard a whimpering sound. Lyn opened her eyes again. Jasper was licking her face and making soothing whining sounds. Huddled tightly into the corner of the hallway, Lyn stared, wide-eyed and petrified. Jasper wanted her to move. His instinct had told him that something wasn't right with her. If only he could speak. Jasper barked at Lyn, loudly. He barked again. Lyn jumped, snapped out of her spell-bound world and grabbed Jasper. She held him tightly, still shaking from her strange vision.

When Stan returned home early, Lyn leapt into his arms.

'Well, honey, what have I done to deserve such a loving welcome?'

'I just love you, that's all.'

Stan gave his wife a loving kiss and kicked off his shoes. He turned to see Lyn wandering back towards the kitchen.

'Coffee?' She asked.

'I'd love one, thanks.'

Stan's brown eyes darted to the left. His brain had sensed something. His unconscious mind playing tricks? A sixth sense telling him to look to the left? His extrasensory perception made him look straight into the painting. His eyes widened, his mouth fell open.

'Sweetheart, come here,' he called. Lyn noticed a hint of anxiety in his trembling voice.

'What is it, love?'

'Look at this – in the painting.'

Lyn remained motionless – as if she were caught in a frozen moment – like a snapshot. She did not take another step.

Stan remained motionless as he looked deep into the graveyard. There was a gravestone, prominent and fresh. His name was inscribed upon it.

'Why is my name on a gravestone?'

Lyn did not answer.

'Lyn?'

He turned away to face his wife.

Lyn screamed. Jasper barked. Lyn backed away into the kitchen as Jasper began to growl fiercely.

'What is it?' Stan asked.

He crept, slowly into the living room, keeping an eye on the angry Retriever. He didn't recognise Jasper – he wasn't the same dog. Jasper had never growled at anyone before.

Stan turned to face the mirror and screamed loudly, something that he'd never done. But what he saw in the mirror was horrific. There was a face – it was his all right, but where was his skin? Stan put his hand to his cheek and felt the blood. The remaining skin fell away, revealing raw muscle and tissue. His eyes were bloodshot red. Then the image in the mirror began to laugh, like a demonic beast. Stan closed his eyes tightly.

'Get away from me! Whoever you are,' he screamed. 'Lyn – help me, please, someone help me!'

Stan collapsed onto the floor. He felt Jasper licking his face, and he heard Lyn – her calming words began to settle him.

'Stan, sweetheart, can you hear me?'

Stan opened his eyes. 'Look at me, what has happened to my face?'

'My love,' said Lyn, softly. 'There is nothing wrong with your face. You are still my handsome husband.'

'What happened?' Stan said, feeling his face with both hands.

'One moment you were agreeing to coffee – the next moment you were collapsed on the floor – right here in the living room, screaming.'

'Jesus, I don't know what came over me.'

Lyn helped him up.

'Jasper was growling at me.'

'No he wasn't,' Lyn replied. 'He was sat here in the kitchen with me. Then we both rushed in to find you here.' Lyn guided him into the kitchen and handed him the coffee. She noticed his hands trembling. The coffee mug shook as if hit by an earthquake.

'Stan,' Lyn said quietly. 'I think I know what happened. Something similar happened to me this afternoon.'

'Like what?'

'I looked into the painting and suddenly found myself witnessing the sacrifice of Jasper. There was some ancient priest speaking in Latin.'

'I saw,' Stan tried to stop his voice from quavering. 'I saw a gravestone with my name on it, then I spoke to you…'

'No you didn't Stan.'

'Well, I thought I spoke to you – about the gravestone. Then I looked in the mirror and saw my face with no skin on it, like from one of those old horror movies we used to watch.'

Lyn gulped down some coffee, noisily. 'Get rid of that paining.'

'It's not the painting. I think it has something to do with that guy Raymond.'

'Why do you say that?'

'Well, he's into all this psycho stuff, paranormal activities. Maybe he has put a spell on us.'

'Oh come on, you don't really believe that stuff do you?'

'I don't know what to believe. All I know is that we have both just had weird, scary visions. Visions that seemed real. And I don't like it. Where's that scotch?'

# Chapter Eight

## Losing mind

When Melissa and Reuben returned home from school, they found their parents sitting in silence at the kitchen table. Stan rested his elbows upon the smooth pine veneer.

'Wassup?' Reuben asked. There was no reply.

'Hey,' Melissa dropped her bag onto the hallway carpet and continued. 'Never guess what we studied in biology?' She waited for a response.

'What?' Lyn asked, slightly unenthusiastically.

'The human brain.'

'Very nice.'

'Mum, did you know that neurotransmitters are the key to all of your bodily functions?'

'I do now.'

'Well actually, that's not entirely correct. You see, they activate receptors and did you know that serotonin is necessary for appetite, sleep, memory…'

'Melissa,' Stan growled. 'Enough, okay. Your mother and I are not in the mood for lectures about the human anatomy.'

'It's not the anatomy it's…'

'All right, please.'

'Thanks, Dad,' Reuben said. 'I've had this lecture all the way home.'

'Your loss,' announced Melissa, as she picked up the bag and sauntered upstairs. 'By the way,' she called. 'Raymond is coming round to help me with my homework.'

'No he isn't,' Stan snapped. 'I don't think that's a good idea.'

Melissa was now in her room. She shouted back downstairs, 'Why not?'

'Because I said so.'

Lyn raised herself slowly off the chair. She had been sitting there for so long she thought she had been glued to it. Something caught her eye. 'Reuben?'

No answer.

'Reuben, get away from that painting.'

'Why?'

'Because.'

'Because what?'

'Because I say so.'

It was too late. Reuben spotted an interesting piece of artwork. 'Have you studied this painting? Every time I look at it I see something else. It's like…' He hesitated. '…it's like the painting is talking to us.'

'What the hell are you going on about?'

Inside the graveyard, on each tombstone were strange markings. He studied the words. 'What does *infernum manet* mean?'

Then he looked closer. One of the church stain-glass windows had an image of a face. 'My God!'

'What is it?' Melissa called. 'Have you found a brain?'

Reuben ignored his sister. 'Mum, Dad, come and look at this.'

Reluctantly, Lyn and Stan joined their son, without looking at the picture.

Reuben spoke without looking at his parents. 'Who painted a picture of me in the church window?'

There was no answer.

'It's not funny.'

Lyn cautiously turned her head towards the evil

57

painting, her eyes barely making contact with the image. She held her breath and slowly allowed her eyes to focus in on the church. There was no face in the stain-glass window. She then glanced quickly at the grave stones. There were no words upon them.

Melissa called down. 'I've just looked up those words you said just now. You know – *infernum manet* – it means **hell awaits** or something. Nice hey. Whoever painted that picture was a bit weird.'

'He is here,' said Reuben, without emotion. 'The man, Dexter, is here, with us. He spoke to me.'

Reuben remained at the painting, eyes focused. As he studied the mystical image, something moved. He peered deeply into the graveyard. He felt cold, felt a presence. There was a strong power drawing him in, an eerie silence followed. His eyes rolled up to the window, the face was there again. Suddenly the weathered old face lurched towards him, right out of the frame. '*Help me*,' the voice screamed.

Reuben stumbled back onto the stairs.

'Reuben?'

No answer. He sat motionless on the second stair.

Melissa glided down the stairs and sat close. 'You okay?'

'Hey? Ah, yeah, I'm okay. That image, the face, came right out at me. I heard it shout "help me," really weird.'

'Right,' Stan shouted. 'That does it. This painting goes.'

'Oh why?' yelled Melissa.

'Because it's playing mind-tricks on us, that's why.'

'Dad, I didn't think you believed all that stuff.'

'I don't, well, I do, I don't know.'

Melissa re-entered her bedroom and picked up her mobile phone. She scrolled down to Raymond.

'Hi, Raymond, it's Melissa.....yeah. I'm fine thanks, um, I was wondering – could you come round tonight?' She waited for his response. 'Great, but, um, meet me outside – by the gate. Mum and Dad are freaking out over this painting.'

Raymond spoke up, 'What do you mean *freaking out*?'

'Just get here as soon as poss, yeah?'

'I'll come over now.'

'See ya,' Melissa disconnected the call and sat down clumsily on her bed, knocking off a soft toy. She bent down and picked up Boo-boo the bear. 'What's going on?' she asked the soft toy. She looked into Boo-boo's beady eyes. For a moment there, she thought she saw him blink. Melissa's heart skipped a beat.

Stan began to loosen the painting's fixings. 'Jesus!'

'Don't tell me,' Lyn remarked. 'You've burnt yourself.'

Stan studied his fingers. 'Damn thing.'

'I'll take it down,' Reuben demanded. 'It trusts me.'

'What the hell are you talking about?'

'Dad, just let me do it.'

Reuben began to remove the painting from its fixings. He did not feel the burning – it was not hot to the touch.

'Why is it only me that gets burnt?' Stan asked.

'Because, Dad, you never wanted it in the first place. The painting doesn't like you.'

'Oh, come on Reuben, don't talk rubbish.'

'I'm not.'

'Anyway, what was it that your sister said – those words you saw – death awaits.'

'Hell awaits, actually.'

'Well, either way, it sounds like the painting doesn't like you either.' Stan spoke with a wry grin.

Melissa grabbed her light jacket and slipped on a pair of shoes. She popped Booboo up by her pillow and turned to leave the bedroom. She stopped. As she turned her head back towards the bear, Booboo's head turned. Melissa stared at the bear, looked away and then back to the soft toy again. His head was straight. 'Freaking weird,' she muttered.

Melissa crept downstairs, sneaked past the living room where the others were all contemplating what to do with the painting, and out through the door.

Raymond was arriving in perfect time. She rushed up to him and grabbed his hand. 'Something weird is happening – it's all since we got that painting.'

'I know,' Raymond declared. 'I felt a presence when I was here yesterday. And that picture of you – the family pic – I saw it move.'

'It moved?'

'I didn't say anything cos' I guessed you'd think I was crazy. Then your dad saw it was askew – then he burnt his fingers on the new painting…'

'Yeah I know that bit, but listen – some weird stuff has happened – Mum and Dad are acting strange, Reuben is seeing things in the painting and…'

'Seeing what?'

'He sees a face in the church window, something jumped out at him and on each gravestone he sees words – hell awaits – written in Latin.'

'Why Latin?'

'How should I know?'

'Let me take a look at the painting.'

'Do you think that's a good idea?'

'Melissa – there's something not right here, I'll take a look – after all, I do study the weird and unusual.'

'You can say that again. In fact, you *are* weird and unusual,' said Melissa grinning.

60

'Well, thanks!'

Raymond entered the house slowly and quietly. Why he moved so stealthily he did not know. Lyn and Stan could see him coming in, and why would he need to keep quiet? After all, it was just an oil painting.

'Hello Mr and Mrs Thorne.'

Lyn and Stan remained silent. They did not feel like inviting him in.

Raymond turned, slowly, knelt down and faced the painting that was now on the floor. He studied the detail of the brush strokes, the wonderful blend of colours, and the extraordinary accuracy.

'This church,' he said, pointing. 'It's a local church – isn't it that church in Hamden Heath?'

'The Heath?' Melissa asked. 'That's where dad works.'

'Well,' Stan piped up, 'Wherever or whatever, the painting has to go.'

'Do not move this painting – it cannot be moved.'

'Why on earth not?'

'Mr Thorne, you said *why on earth*. It may not be *on* earth – more likely – *under* it.'

'So, you're telling me that this piece of junk is alive, and that it doesn't want to leave?'

'Not quite. You see, Stan, there have been numerous recordings over the years of paranormal phenomenon when –'

'Please,' Stan interrupted. 'Less lecture, more fact.'

'Well, it's,' Raymond paused and looked around the tidy living room, deliberately failing to make eye contact. 'You see, the paranormal isn't just about ghosts and haunting. In fact, most of the time it's to do with the mind – using our extra senses and sometimes playing tricks on us – but,' he paused again, scanned the room as if checking that nobody else was listening.

'Occasionally trapped souls need to find a way out.'

'You really do believe this rubbish, don't you?'

'Dad, listen to what he has to say,' Melissa demanded. 'He knows more about this than we do.'

'Yeah – too much – in fact, I think that you have somehow, and I quote, played mind tricks on us.'

'Dad –'

'It's okay, Melissa. Raymond touched her shoulder with an instant calming effect. 'Your father has a right to express opinion. At the moment we don't know what is going on. Let me just say that I have nothing to do with it.'

'Oh yeah,' Stan pulled-up aggressively close to Raymond and looked the lad square in his face. 'Then tell us what the heck is going on. I tell you something, until you come up with a logical reason for all this, then I will assume you have something to do with it. Oh, and believe me, if I find out you've been playing some weird psycho-voodoo-hypnosis then God damn you I'll…'

'Mr Thorne – you may have already been damned. If by what I have seen is anything to go by, I'd say that there is certainly an unhappy entity or disturbed energy.'

'Take your mumbo-jumbo rubbish and get out.'

'Dad!' Melissa yelled. 'I thought you studied religion at uni, you should have an open mind.'

'It's all right, Melissa.' Raymond turned to leave. Without looking back at Stan, he spoke. 'Mr Thorne – I can help you. If you change your mind then call me. Melissa will pass on my number.'

Melissa spoke an almost silent goodbye, and then turned to face her father. 'Thanks, Dad,' she said angrily and stormed upstairs to her bedroom.

# Chapter Nine

## Demons inside

## Tuesday

'Mr Thorne.'

Stan remained where he was. His eyes were bloodshot from lack of sleep. His transfixed stare like that of a man lost in his own dream.

'Mr Thorne,' the voice was louder this time – more determined to catch his attention.

Stan jumped. He looked to his right to see one of Terry Hatchet's printers, from next door; Simon.

Terry Hatchet ran the small printing company that was adjacent to the paper mill. They were as good as partners – Stan produced the paper, Terry ran the print. The two small companies were local concerns – that is, local labour, local raw material and also very little product went out of the local vicinity. There were daily visits by passing tourists and anyone with a general interest in old heritage would stop by and pay a fee to have a guided tour. The small fee for tours around the establishments helped considerably with the ever-increasing costs – the traditional methods were no match for the cheap factory chains, so opening up to the tourist trade made financial sense. Initially, the traditional mill was saved from closure by local interest groups and a concerned local politician. The local newspapers were printed there, plus most of Hamden district school paper, advertising flyers and occasionally on-demand paperback books. Terry, who ran the local printers, persuaded his old school-friend, Stan, to run the mill. Back then, Stan had little experience with running a mill; in fact, he had none at all. His background was factory farming, so there were some transferable skills. The paper and print were run under two names –**The Old Mill Paper Company** and **Hamden Print**. Stan and Terry had wondered about changing the names to a single concern of Hatchet and Thorne, but they concluded that this sounded rather too much like a high street solicitors.

It was an idyllic setting and a great place to work. The traditional water mill with its country settings was most picturesque – like a classic Constable work of art on a live canvass; a perfect painting. From the mill, and past the red-brick Victorian building that was home to Hamden Print, was a light meadow that acted as a foreground to the church. There were just three regular workers in each company, which made for friendly working environments. In addition, a lady from the village, Valerie, organised the public tours and ran the little kiosk that sold light snacks. Tours themselves, would be led by Terry. All happy workers.

Occasionally, Reverend Harris would wander down to say hello, have a gossip, a cup of Earl Grey tea and one or two scones that Valerie had prepared earlier.

Now, Tuesday would normally have been quiet – not much happened on Tuesdays; run-of-the-mill stuff; pun intended. Tuesdays saw new stock of recycled Spruce and Pine pulp, weekly delivery of chemicals and a few flyers were normally run-off at the printers. But this Tuesday was different.

'Mr Thorne, Terry wants to see you.'

Stan slid back his chair on the stone surface, making a grating sound. He stood up and stretched. 'What's it about?'

'Dunno,' came the reply from the young printer.

'You wanted to see me, Terry?'

'Ah, yes, thanks for coming round. Stan, take a seat.'

'I'd rather stand actually – I seem to have been sitting all day.'

'Well, anyway, it's this,' Terry took a breath and breathed out slowly. He pulled a facial expression that showed an air of awkwardness. 'What do you make of this?' Terry handed Stan a single sheet of paper. It was blank.

'Can't see anything on it, looks good quality. Anything wrong with the paper?'

'Oh no, no. Paper's fine.' Terry sighed. 'Stan, what's with the watermark?'

'Watermark? I haven't produced paper with a watermark for some time...'

'I know,' Terry stopped him. 'Stan, I know that we only produce watermarked paper on demand. Take another look.'

Stan looked carefully into the paper. Through the fibrous grain, he could see the words;

### *Mors Expectet*

Stan looked on with intrigue. 'Latin?'

Terry looked him in the eyes, brushed aside his overgrown fringe and stated; 'Death Awaits. It's on the whole batch you supplied. Not something we can do anything about – apart from make some horror comics, maybe.'

'I'll talk to the two lads – see if they know

anything.'

'Stan, I've known you for a long time. I know that you wouldn't run a practical joke like this – not at today's costs. Have a talk to the lads.'

'I will.' Stan began to leave the office.

'Oh, and Stan, are you feeling all right? You don't seem yourself, and you look a little pasty.'

'I'm okay,' Stan replied.

Stan could not find an answer to the strange watermark. The two lads who ran the production machines had sworn innocence. Stan believed them whole-heartedly. There was a lot more to this weirdness than met the eye.

Back home, that evening, Stan confronted his wife. He sat her down and spoke uneasily. 'Lyn, we had a batch of paper with an unusual watermark. It said *death awaits*, in Latin. Terry asked me about it – he found it in the paper they were going to use to produce some flyers for one of the shops in the village. What's going on?'

'Who made the mark?'

'Nobody…well nobody that we know, anyway.'

'Someone is really screwing with us,' Lyn said solemnly. 'This is just getting out of hand. Whoever this is, needs to stop messing us up.'

'Someone, or *something*, Lyn.'

Lyn nodded. 'Something has got inside of our minds – making us see horrible things and do crazy stuff.'

'You think I put that watermark in the paper, don't you?'

Lyn gave a moment to think. 'I'm not saying that you knew you were doing it, maybe you were…' She couldn't work out how to finish the sentence, so Stan did it for her.

'Maybe I was possessed? Could Raymond be right?'

'Do you want me to call him?'

Stan nodded slowly. 'Yes.'


Raymond came to the house straight away. Stan apologised for being disrespectful and impolite the evening before. Raymond accepted the apology without fuss and without a grudge.

'Let me see the paper, Mr Thorne.'

Melissa and Reuben had joined them.

'I see,' Raymond said, studying the paper with a magnifying glass. 'And you say that you have no recollection of doing this?'

Stan gave a half nod.

'And nobody else at the mill had done it?'

'They said they knew nothing about it, and anyway, I would normally see what they were doing. Normally.'

'And the printers?'

'The chap that runs it is a very good friend. I'd know if he was lying. He said that the watermark was already in the paper when it was delivered.'

'Who delivered it?'

'I did. First thing.'

'So the batch was produced yesterday?'

Stan looked at Raymond and nodded.

Raymond told the family to stay put and disappeared back home. Ten minutes later, he returned with a small briefcase.

Four sets of questioning eyes watched Raymond open the briefcase and remove a scientific kit.

'Are you really just a student?' Lyn asked. 'You look a bit like a mad scientist.'

'I am. Well, not mad, but parapsychology is a science. It's not all about summoning up ghosts!' He grinned broadly. 'What I have here is a little test. I am going to use this little EVP recorder first; this'll search all the white noise and faint background voice throughout the frequencies.'

Lyn gave a bewildered look towards her husband.

'Electronic voice phenomena,' Raymond stated. He scanned the four observers. 'I can see you guys are a little baffled. Not to worry, so was I at first.'

'How long have you been doing this?' Stan asked.

'I've studied the paranormal since my early teens and two years at university.'

Melissa watched Raymond with quiet awe. Everything he did, everything he said, was inching closer to her heart. Melissa felt that he was more than just a friend – feelings of which she had not felt before.

'You're so knowledgeable,' Melissa remarked. 'I bet you've done this loads of times, yeah?'

'Actually it's my first time.'

Stan and Lyn stole glances. They were understandably apprehensive. What was this guy about to do?

'Raymond,' Stan said. 'I thought you were going to see how this paper managed to get a weird watermark. What's the point of a voice recorder?'

'Firstly I want to check for any local presence. You know, see if there is something in the house.'

'Oh, right.'

'I'll need you all to sit down and make sure that you are comfortable. Switch off all mobile phones. Oh, Mrs Thorne – would you kindly mute the landline phone and make sure the dog is asleep in the kitchen – and shut the door.'

When Lyn had checked on Jasper and muted the phone, she spoke quietly. 'I really don't know what you are doing, Raymond – please don't do some kind of séance.'

'It's all right. This is not a true séance, Mrs Thorne. All I am testing for are spiritual sounds.'

'I don't like the sound of that.'

'Mrs Thorne, you are quite right to feel a bit nervy, but believe me it is safe.'

'How do you know – you said yourself that this is the first time.'

'Trust me.'

Raymond popped in a set of earphones and switched on the device, closed his eyes and listened. After five minutes of complete silence, Lyn began to fidget. Raymond opened his eyes. He glanced around at the others. He could see that they were unwilling to continue.

'Okay,' Raymond said, removing his earphones and switching off the device. 'I haven't picked up any unusual noise. I guess there's nothing here. Now I'll check that paper.'

Raymond placed his hand firmly onto the paper and closed his eyes again. His powerful concentration radiated out across the living room. Two minutes passed and he opened his eyes. 'Nothing.'

Then Raymond reached into his case and picked up a small bottle, poured some clear liquid all over the paper and then explained what he was doing. 'This is called Ninhyndrin – it bonds with the amino acid from fingerprints, thus showing them up in a blue colour.'

'Yes, all very well,' Stan added, 'But all that will do is show our fingerprints – yours, mine and Terry's.'

'That's right, Mr Thorne. But any other prints – non-human for example, will show up as a faint green.'

They waited. Raymond studied the paper with an odd-looking pair of glasses, over his own specs. Apparently the glasses helped to reduce ambient artificial light and solar UV, allowing clearer observation of the contaminated surface.

'There's nothing more than human prints – three different sets.'

'So your experiments are, shall we say, non-conclusive?'

'Not exactly, you see, I have ruled out the presence of a household entity, and also that the paper has not been touched by anyone other than us.'

'So,' Stan dropped his head. 'I was the one who made the watermark.'

'Yes, Mr Thorne. You were unaware that you produced the marking because you were, for want of a better word, possessed.'

Lyn looked at Raymond with intrigue. 'You seem to know a lot, that's one thing, but where did you get this fancy scientific stuff from?'

'The ghost kit? Sort of borrowed it from the lab. I've been waiting so long for an opportunity to use it. This is great.'

'Great for you.' Reuben finally had something to bring to the get-together. 'Not great for us. We've seen weird visions, strange things inside the painting and Dad's had his fingers' burnt. Not great. Raymond – you reckon the painting is possessed?'

Raymond nodded. 'There's one way to find out. The painting may have been physically touched by the spirit that's possibly within it. Tonight we do a séance.'

# Chapter Ten

## The writing is on the wall

The family settled down together in the quiet living room, rather apprehensively. Stan had fought hard to convince himself that this was the right thing to do. As a true non-believer of dark arts, the forty-three year old had never seen any type of séance or met any sort of psychic.

Raymond positioned the painting onto the large wooden oval table that had been cleared of any family items. Next he made sure that all five of them were seated comfortably, and spaced equally around the table. In front of each member, he lit small, non-aromatic candles. Five candles in all. ☆

'I want each of you to place your hands very gently upon the painting. This will combine our energy. Go on, do it now. I am going to attempt to speak to the person who painted this. All we have is his name.'

Melissa felt cold. With her voice slightly trembling, she asked, 'Do you think that it's the painter of the picture who has been doing these weird things?'

'It's all we have, Melissa.'

'I'm scared,' she replied, looking straight into Raymond's eyes.'

'No need to be. All I'm going to do is try to establish communication – have a quick chat if he wishes to.'

'But that's assuming that he is dead, right?' Reuben asked.

'Yes. If this man Dexter isn't dead, we obviously can't talk to him. Well, not this way. Now we could summon up some other kind of spirit via the painting, though.'

Apprehension and nervousness cut through the air like a silent tornado.

'Don't tell me, Raymond,' Stan said with his head down. 'This is your first time?'

'Yep. Right let's begin. Close your eyes.'

With the recording equipment set up, Raymond turned off the lights and sat with the others, forming the fifth point of a star.

*'Dexter Manning. Ego invocabo te.'*

Melissa opened an eye and glanced sideways at Raymond. She then opened her other eye and let her eyes wander across the others. They too, had open eyes. The question upon all their faces was 'How is this guy speaking a form of ancient Latin? And WHY?'

'Dexter. Rise up from within your painting, resurgemus, there shall be no purgatory. Liber es. You are free. Liber es. Let us feel your presence and share with us your pain.'

Reuben almost spoke out aloud, but refrained and spoke within his mind. 'I'd rather not share your pain.'

'Rise, Dexter. What is it that you desire? We shall give you all that you wish for.'

Stan spoke under his breath. 'Not such a great idea.'

Lyn laughed silently, then the more she tried not to laugh, the more she needed to. Trying to hold back the laughter was harder than stopping a runaway train.

'Mrs Thorne,' Raymond said. 'Please. If you wish

not to continue then we must break this link. If you would like my help, please refrain from laughing.'

Melissa looked across at her with a glare.

'He's right,' Reuben said. 'Let's get on with it.'

Lyn, with straightened face, apologised and allowed Raymond to start all over again.

They remained quiet and obedient, but the negative atmosphere was impossible to work with. Raymond was just about to call it a day when something happened;

The candles flickered, the flames danced in perfect rhythms. Then they all went out.

Nobody spoke.

Nobody took a breath.

Then the flames came back, flickering and casting long, faint shadows across the walls. Then the candle in front of Stan went out with a faint hiss and a wisp of smoke, as if it had been pinched by moist fingers. Now, Stan was a believer. From then on, he was a believer. But why had *his* candle gone out. Was this a sign?

Raymond spoke again.

'Is that you, Dexter?'

There were no other signs of activity.

'If that is you, Dexter, give me a sign. Let us feel your presence. If that is you, Dexter, extinguish the candle that is before me.'

There was a long silence. They waited with baited breath. Time seemed to stand still. An old clock could be heard, distant at first, then stronger and louder. The ticking was slow – a metronomic pendulum in slow motion. Raymond could see an image in his mind. He could see an old grandfather clock, some paintings – a Van Gough picture and there was a rocking chair – empty, but still rocking gently.

The candle in front of Raymond went out.

Raymond felt his mind fill with rushing images; all sorts of things darting to and fro – many images of an unhappy soul. He could hear a voice within his head but could not make out the words.

'Ahh! No.' Raymond broke the chain. 'Please, Dexter, you must return. Thank you for your...' He felt terrific pains racing through his head. His mind was awash with painful images that jabbed his brain like sharpened knives. 'No, Dexter, please, I beg you to leave this place, return to the side of which you belong.'

Raymond pulled out his ear plugs, stood up, the chair toppled over and he collapsed onto the floor.

'Raymond,' Melissa screamed. Lyn turned on the lights. Stan disappeared into the kitchen for a glass of water for Raymond, and a sneaky scotch for himself, which he downed in one.

But still sitting was Reuben. His eyes were wide open like huge black saucers. Stan offered the water to Raymond, who sipped it graciously. Then they all looked at Reuben as he began to speak.

'I will, Mr Manning, I will see to it.'

'See to what?' Lyn asked, rising up from the floor. Reuben – what are you saying?'

Reuben's eyes refocused on the table. Then his head fell forward.

'Hold him,' Lyn shouted.

Stan and Melissa supported Reuben as he remained unconscious. But it lasted just a few seconds.

'What just happened?' Reuben asked, in a dreamy state. 'Where am I?'

Raymond suggested that they all get some rest and refrain from thinking about things too much, but that was easier said than done;

The lights went out, all of them. A cool whistle of air brushed past. The other electrical appliances stopped.

'Oh very funny Reuben.'

'Mum, it wasn't me.'

Lyn struggled to see in the dark. 'Melissa?'

'Nobody turned off the power.'

'Then how did everything stop,' Stan added. 'How did the lights just go out?'

Lyn felt Melissa's hand grip hers tightly.

'Mum, I'm scared.' Melissa could see enough to work out a shape; that of a human, sitting in one of the dining chairs. 'There's someone sat at the table.'

Stan crept forward, straining his eyes in the darkness. There was definitely someone sat there. A man. The chair was facing away.

'Dad,' Reuben whispered. 'Don't get too close.'

Stan ignored the warning and continued, creeping slowly. He moved closer, closer. His hand moved up towards the figure, about to touch the shoulder.

The figure leapt up, twisting to face Stan. The chair toppling backwards. The shape was of human form, yet it was not entirely..... human. The face lit up brightly, an evil demonic entity. It lurched towards Stan violently, arms stretched, long pointed fingers with razor-sharp nails. The wide-open mouth exposed a long thin black tongue.

Stan, stumbling back, saw deep into the creature's eyes. Pure evil, malevolent evil.

'Aaargh!' he cried. 'What the hell.'

Lyn grabbed the twins and rushed them out through the door, Raymond followed with Stan running quickly behind.

The lights came on. All the power restored.

They huddled together in the kitchen, barely

breathing, trembling like autumn leaves.

'Okay,' Lyn said. Her voice trembling. 'Who on earth was that?'

'Not *who* but *what*.' Stan replied. 'Let me take a look.'

'You crazy?' Lyn grabbed his arm. 'You can't go back in there.'

'Look, the lights are on, power is on. I'm sure whatever that thing was, is gone.'

Stan crept back into the living room, brushing up close to the wall as he went. 'Nothing here. Chair has fallen over. We definitely didn't imagine that. Did we?'

There could be no denying it. They all saw the dark image of someone, something, in the chair. They agreed that it was not in their collective imagination.

'Right,' said Stan. 'We get someone to sort this out.'


Raymond went back to his parent's place and crept up to his bedroom. He began to check the readings from the recording device. There was a lot of static, crackling and white-noise. But there were also words spoken, in deep, whispered tones. The words were Latin. They said;

# Infernum manet.

The night air had been humid and still. Lyn tossed and turned in bed and felt as tired in the morning as she did seven hours ago.

Stan yawned, stretched, and took note of the time. 'Oh God, I've slept through the alarm clock. Damn it, it's gone eight o'clock.' He stumbled out of bed like a worn-out zombie. He gasped. 'Lyn!' Stan screamed her name out like a school teacher about to discipline a naughty student. 'What the hell is this,' he waved his hand across the bedroom wall.

Lyn sat bolt upright in bed. She allowed her tired eyes to roam the peach wall. 'That's my handwriting.'

'I can see that,' Stan announced with his hands on his hips. 'Are you going to tell me what this is?'

Lyn could barely speak. She could not recall doing it. When did she scrawl Latin words all over the wallpaper?

'What does it all mean?' Stan asked, calmly.

Lyn continued to stare, not study. She had a look of guilt and bewilderment. When she spoke again, the words were muttered slowly, and in a deep voice.

'*Melissa aeterna pro Morax. Lyn servus pro Morax. Stan sacrificium pro Puer ab Lilith. Reuben sacrificium pro Vapula.* I have never studied Latin, Stan. Never in my life – but I know what this means.'

'What does it mean, then?' Stan moved up to the main wall, slamming his palm against the writing. 'What the freaking hell is going on?'

'Well, Stan, that is precisely what's going on – hell.'

'Oh for goodness sake. Just tell me what it means.'

'It's all jumbled up and some words are different. But basically we are all to be sacrificed.'

'Well I'm glad that's cleared up,' Stan said, with a hint of sarcasm. 'If you need me, I'll be downstairs.'

Whilst Stan raced to get ready for work, Lyn continued to study the wall. Other words were neatly written in a perfect pattern.

*Quinque spiritu.* **Melissa** *aeterna pro Morax. vitam aeterna. quinque spiritus diaboli.*
**Lyn** *servus pro Morax es* **Raymond** *sacrificium Satanas supra inferna est.*
**Reuben** *sec* **Stan** *infernum in omni aeternum.*

*Dominos Vestros - Morax, Vapula, Azazel, Puer ab Lilith, Dominus Luciferi.*

Lyn had no recollection. She had no idea why the names were written between the words in bold. There were also strange names that meant very little to her.

'We need to call Raymond.'

Stan called back up the stairs. 'No we don't. it's Raymond who has done this.'

'Oh come on – how has he done this? Do you think he came into the room whilst we slept?'

'Either that or he has cursed us all.'

'Oh go to work, Stanley. And watch what you print.'

Stan muttered under his breath and walked out of the house. He dodged the rain as he approached the car. Once inside, he looked up through the window at the heavy morning sky. 'What's in store for me today, I wonder?'

Nothing unusual happened at work. Stan knew that there were watchful and judgemental eyes burning into

78

him.

'What?'

'Sorry, nothing,' replied one of the young workers.

'Well stop looking at me like that.' Stan sighed, turned off the chemical mixer and twisted on his feet. He looked straight at the two lads. 'What's on your mind?'

'Nothing.'

'All right, I know what is on your mind and the answers to your questions are simple. Yes I did put that retched watermark in the paper and no I don't remember doing it. If you must know, I've had a bad couple of days.'

'Maybe you should see a doctor, Mr Thorne.'

'Maybe *you* should get back to work.'


Stan studied the chemicals swirling slowly within the vat. 'How are we going to get out of this hell,' he wondered.

# Chapter Eleven

## Ghostly things

## Thursday 12<sup>th</sup>

'Why have I not had any strange visions?'

Melissa looked up from her morning mug of coffee. 'I mean, you lot have seen horrible things and done weird stuff, like, you know, been taken over, or whatever it's called? Why hasn't it happened to me?'

'Your time will come.' The voice came from behind her – gruff and whispered. She even felt the breath down her neck.

'Oh very funny, Reuben.'

'What?' Her brother blurted out whilst still in the bathroom.

Melissa spun her head and looked around, scanning the kitchen like a hawk. 'Who said that?'

'Said what?' Lyn replied. 'Nobody said anything.'

'I could have sworn someone…'

'Reuben, hurry up – your porridge is getting cold. And eaten. Stan don't eat his breakfast.'

'I'm hungry.'

'Stan, you, oh, forget it.'

Lyn hurried through the usual morning procedures of sandwich-making for the three kids, as she would often call them. Three grown up kids, unable to complete even the slightest morning chore of making lunch. She didn't mind – it was all part of the housewife thing. And there was, of course, the morning kick-up-the-ass for the slow Neanderthal of a son.

Stan looked up from shovelling sweet porridge. 'Don't tempt fate, Melissa. Do not speak too soon. You asked why nothing has happened to you? Well don't ask. And that word you're looking for – not taken over – it's possessed.'

'So you really *believe* do you Dad?'

'How can I *not* believe? You tell me. We haven't imagined all this – you saw the candles go out and re-ignite. You can't deny seeing that.....thing, in the chair. We all saw it.'

Melissa put the mug down gently then ran her finger around the rim slowly. 'Actually, I didn't say before, but Monday evening I thought I saw...'

Lyn and Stan both looked at her with eager anticipation.

'I guess you think I'm crazy but I saw my old cuddly bear blink and turn its head.'

Lyn swallowed hard. 'Like those old Hollywood horror movies?' She noticed Reuben saunter into the kitchen. This time she did not say 'about time' or 'better late than never.' Lyn said nothing.

'Morning,' Reuben uttered. He did not get a reply.

'Right,' Lyn said. 'We are getting a proper medium, or a qualified psychic in. I have had enough of this.'

With a mouthful of porridge, Stan added, 'Why don't we just remove the painting – we all seem to agree that it's the painting that has caused all this fuss.'

Melissa spoke up. 'Hear me out – I'll have Raymond find someone – somebody with some more experience. I'll get on it right away.'

Melissa rushed upstairs, settled onto the bed and turned Boo-boo the soft toy to face away. She called Raymond. 'Do you know of anyone who can help? My parents want to chuck the painting; bad idea?'

'Yes, Melissa. Try not to let them remove it.

Disturbing the painting may anger the spirit. Listen, I can't promise anything but there's a man called Raphael – he's an Italian psychic. Actually, he's been a priest, a scientist, a lecturer, a medium and psychic. He will help you.'

'How do you know him?'

'He gave a talk at university – he was amazing.'

'Italian?'

'Yeah, from Vatican City. His full name is Enoch Raphael. His name is very meaningful – and they say it's his real name, too.'

'I don't care about his name – just get him here.'

A short time lapsed before Raymond called back. As always, he'd lived up to his promise. It was a pleasant surprise to find someone like him, somebody who actually does what he says he'll do. Melissa had met enough people already in her life to know that few could be trusted to actually carry out a simple task or favour. She truly admired Raymond, or Ray, as she was beginning to call him. He wasn't one of those people who said 'I'll call you,' and then fail to act on it. She couldn't be bothered for them. She *could* be bothered with Ray. Seriously.

'I've managed to get in touch with Enoch – he seems very interested.' Raymond spoke in soft, quiet tones, the sort of voice that carried mystique and charm. Melissa almost melted.

'I can't believe you managed to talk to him – I mean, I *can* believe you called, it's just like you to keep your word.' She stumbled through the words, awkwardly. 'I just can't believe you, he, I mean, Enoch, um,'

She heard Raymond chuckle to himself.

'Oh, just help me out, Ray. You know what I mean.'

'Ray? You've never called me *Ray* before.'

'Haven't I? Um, anyway, Raymond, when can this priest from the Vatican come over?'

'Hold on there, firstly, he *was* a priest, or maybe he still is, anyway his name is Enoch.'

'As in the Bible.'

'Yeah, wow, um, that's good, but that's a whole new story for another time.'

Melissa smiled at the phone, she wasn't sure why. 'You know, my life has been pretty dull up until now – I mean, a few weeks ago I met you, a few days ago we buy some random painting that's haunted and now we get a visit from a guy from Rome. Anything but dull.'

'Oh you make me laugh!' Raymond had to smile back to her. 'Switch to face-view so we can see each other.' They tapped their phones to live feed. 'Now I can see you smile, oh sorry – I bet that sounds like I'm a creepy sort of guy.'

'No, no, I know you're not,' she said. 'Anything but creepy. Lovely, I mean...' Melissa smacked her forehead. She needed to come up with something fast; 'That sounded bad – shall we just forget the last two minutes?'

'Sounds like a plan! Now, back to the serious side – Enoch will arrive late this evening.'

'Today is Thursday the twelfth. You know what I said about recent events? Meeting you, the painting, Enoch...' Melissa paused. 'And tomorrow is the thirteenth.'

'Melissa, there is nothing in it – Friday the thirteenth is an old silly superstition that has been moulded into a big Hollywood dough and baked till it's overdone.'

'Oh, that's brilliant!' she laughed. 'But there's something in this – there's just too many weird things happening for all this to be a coincidence. Too weird.'

'Weird?' Raymond questioned. 'Like me?'

'No, silly!'

'Listen,' Raymond put on a thoughtful tone. 'Yes there's been some crazy stuff going on, let's not jump to conclusions, though. But I know what you mean.'

'See? Just like I'm stuck in a science fiction novel. I feel that nothing is real any more. It just feels like I'm in a ghost story. I don't believe in horror stories, Raymond.'

'Melissa, you'd better start – I think we're in one.'

Melissa gave no answer. She pondered on the dark subject for a few seconds before noticing the clock – its glowing red digits telling her that if she doesn't pick herself up and get moving, she's be late for school.

'I've got to go, I've still got to go to school, you know. When can I see you again?'

'I will be over tonight. Seven?'

'I'll see you then.'


A non-motivating and rather tedious day at school had Melissa mentally exhausted by the time she returned home. She informed her parents that Raymond, or *Ray*, was coming round at seven. She decided to freshen up with a nice relaxing bath.

Lyn was preparing dinner. Everything she did was in a robotic, hypnotic state. She was on auto-pilot. Nothing could shake those dreadful images from her mind.

Lyn heard a scream. It was one of those blood-curdling shrieks from an old horror flick.

'Melissa?' Lyn yelled out from the kitchen. 'Melissa?'

'What the hell was that?' Stan asked anxiously.

'It's Melissa.'

Lyn and Stan rushed upstairs.

Inside the bathroom, in the bath, Melissa began to shake, uncontrollably. She looked forward, over a sea of red blood. She stood up, with soapy water cascading down her body. As she stepped out a sixth sense told her to re-examine the bath tub. It was just soapy, frothy, bathwater. Nothing more, nothing less. No blood. She wrapped up in a towel.

'Melissa? Are you all right?' Stan's voice was ripe with concern. 'Honey, are you okay?'

Trembling, Melissa managed to reply. 'Yeah, I thought I saw something, that's all.'

'That's all?' Stan replied. 'You scream the house down and then dismiss it?'

Melissa positioned her feet onto the dry bathmat, and faced the mirror. The rectangular mirror was as misted up as a November morning. She gazed into the opaque glass and fixed her eyes onto infinity. With a wet hand, she slowly began to clear the moisture from the glass in an arc.

She screamed, again, and again.

Stan tugged at the bathroom door-handle. 'Melissa, unlock the door, Melissa.'

With her feet frozen to the soggy bathmat, Melissa panted short quick breaths. Tension flared inside her chest so tight that she thought she would stop breathing.

'Melissa, please,' Lyn cried.

'I'm gonna kick the door in,' Stan declared. 'On the count of three, Melissa, sweetheart, stand back, I'm coming in. Melissa?'

No answer.

'One,'

Lyn cupped her hands over her mouth in fear of what she may find behind the closed door.

'Two.'

Melissa peered into the reflection. Through the

blurred moisture came a face. It was hers all right, but it was the image behind her that was far more pressing. There was a ghostly face – an old man's face. The face suddenly lurched forward, over her shoulder – it seemed to escape the bounds of the mirror and lunge towards her.

'Three.'

Stan threw his weight into the door, the simple lock sheared off. The door flung open and with it, out rushed Melissa, dripping wet with water and fear.

She fled past her parents and down the stairs.

Stan, quickly but cautiously, checked the bathroom. There was nothing there but misty air and bathwater.

'Melissa!' Lyn screamed as she gave chase. Stan soon followed.

On no other day would the teenager ever dream of rushing outside wearing just a towel. But this was no ordinary day.

Still panting and screaming she went for the front door. Her hands shook like leaves on a windy autumn day. She fumbled with the lock and handle before swinging the white PVC door against the wall.

'Stop her,' yelled Stan.

Lyn grabbed her hand but the wet skin slipped from her grasp like an eel. Melissa dashed outside into the chilly evening breeze, tripped, and fell.

Lyn came flying up the path with her long overcoat that she fortunately managed to grab on the way out. She helped Melissa up, wrapping her in the coat, tightly, before guiding her back inside the house, upstairs to her bedroom.

'Thank God you caught her when you did, Lyn,' Stan said, calmly. 'God alone knows where she might have gone.'

Just minutes later, Raymond arrived.

Stan looked at the young student with a mixture of feelings – he couldn't determine whether it was admiration, gratitude or concern. 'Please, take a seat. Melissa has had a moment. Would you like a scotch – I'm having one.'

'A moment?'

Lyn ventured back downstairs a while later.

'She's upstairs, resting – I don't think she's going to get any sleep but at least she has calmed down.'

'Did she say what it was all about?' Stan asked, gingerly. He didn't want to push it too far.

'She mumbled something about blood and faces in the mirror – she'll come round in good time.'

Raymond sipped his scotch and placed it back down onto the coaster. 'If it's all right with yourselves, Mr and Mrs Thorne, I'd like to stay tonight. I can crash out down here on the floor – it's not a problem – wouldn't be the first time that I've slept on the floor.'

'Well,' Stan gave thought to the situation. 'I don't think that will be necessary.'

'Stan – why ever not?' Lyn asked. 'Young Raymond here is offering to help. Let's face it – he knows a hell of lot more about what's going on than we do for God's sake.'

Raymond chuckled politely. 'I wish people would stop making similarities with God and Hell! You know, the forces above and below may be a lot closer together than we all might think.'

Stan gave him a quizzical look.

'Mr Thorne,' Raymond paused to take another sip of quality scotch. 'I'm not, as per se, a religious person, but I am open-minded enough to allow myself to study all the facts from all directions. There is something going on here, within this house – within your, I mean, *our* minds – something to do with that painting, no doubt. Let's just wait and see.'

'Wait?' Lyn sat down in the sofa beside her husband. 'What are we waiting for?'

'Enoch Raphael – he's a psychic and medium, amongst many other things. I think the word to describe him is a polym... poly, polymath or something. Anyway, I know him from when he gave a lecture to us at university. He has many years of experience – he'll know what's going on and how we can stop it.'

Stan raised himself up. 'Hang on – a mister *what* do you say?'

'Raphael.'

'So, this Raphael chap – have you invited him here?'

'I am sorry that I did not inform you earlier. But I spoke to him this morning and he said that he was getting the first flight from Rome. To me, that sounds like he's rather concerned.'

'And you've left it until tonight to tell us this?'

'Mr Thorne, I thought by what you said last night that you wanted me to get in touch.'

'Yeah but not just invite him, well, whatever.'

'I can understand your irritation, but believe me, I was coming round to tell you.'

'I'd better check on her,' Lyn said.

'You left her just five minutes ago, Lyn,' Stan reminded her. 'Let her rest.'

'He's right, Mrs Thorne. She has obviously had a scare – seen some kind of scary vision – she needs to rest.'

'All right,' said Lyn. 'You sleep down here tonight. And tomorrow, we shall see what this Raphael has to say.'

'Where did you say he was from?' asked Stan.

'Rome.'

'Well,' Stan said, rising to refresh his glass tumbler.

'Visions straight out of a 1980's horror – a mysterious painting, Latin writing and a priest from Rome.'

He downed another big shot of gulping liquor.

'This has got the whole making for a fine horror movie.'

# Chapter Twelve

## The man from Rome

Enoch Raphael took one look at the British weather and sighed. But the weather was the least of his worries.

'Thank you for flying with us, enjoy your stay.' The stewardess smiled at Enoch and then nodded towards the next passenger. He made his way through the jet-bridge and followed the meandering crocodile of weary travellers into the terminal building. Enoch was tired – it had been a long day. His baggage came along the carousel almost right away. He collected it, then sauntered drearily through the 'nothing-to-declare' green zone and out into the foyer. A man with a sign caught his attention. The sign had his name printed in big bold black letters.

'Hello, I am Mr Raphael.'

'Good evening,' said the chauffeur, noting Enoch's casual clothes, round spectacles, his friendly features and thinning hair. 'Pleased to meet you. May I take your bag?'

'No that won't be necessary, thank you.'

The driver took him out to a nice new BMW and allowed him to settle in. Enoch fell asleep within minutes.

The driver powered down the motorway and onto the dark, mostly unlit b-road. Enoch awoke to some jolting around on a poorly maintained road surface. He rubbed his eyes and glanced out of the side window. A rush of hedgerow dashed past, silhouetted trees raced by, one after another, and occasional farm buildings gave up their hidden positions with glinting lights. The Devonshire country lanes reminded him a little of Tuscany, where he grew up. He smiled at the not-so-subtle differences; there were more hedgerows in Devon, less vineyards, more cows and more rain!

'I am sorry,' he said to the driver. 'I have slept. I'm not such good company.'

'Not a problem, Mr Raphael. You've made the most of the rest, I hope.'

Just then, Enoch spotted the dash clock. 11:40. He had promised Raymond that he would arrive by late evening.

'How much further is it?'

The driver glanced at the on-board navigation. 'Just a few miles,' he said. 'Sorry, kilometres. I forget you Italians work in kilometres.' He grinned into the rear-view mirror. Enoch smiled back.

'Not a problem for me. I'm used to working in miles – I've been to America and England on a few occasions.'

'Oh,' said the driver, nodding to the left. 'Over there is Hamden Heath. It has a beautiful medieval church.'

Enoch nodded. He already knew everything about the church. And he knew who had been buried there.

A few minutes later the car twisted through the narrow lane towards Hamden Village. Enoch was surprised at how many cars passed in the other direction. Back in Tuscany it would be rare to meet another motorist so late in the night. He always felt that England was full of motorists driving around aimlessly at all hours. 'Rome never sleeps, you know. Always cars and motorbikes. But out in the country it is quiet. You English never sleep.'

'You got that right,' said the driver. 'I can guarantee that you'll meet a car in the quietest of places, usually at the most inconvenient position. It's what we call Sod's Law.'

'I have heard of this saying. Yes, we have the same. We say *legge di Murphy.*'

'Well, here we are. This is Pines Avenue....and here's the house.'

'Thank you my friend.' Enoch opened the door. 'Here, thank you for such a pleasant journey.'

'Oh, Mr Raphael, I can't...'

'Nonsense. You must have a tip. In Italy it is customary. Everywhere in the world it is customary. It is about time you English started to tip. Take it.'

'Thank you,' said the driver. He folded up the fifty pound note and slid it into his pocket. This was very unusual indeed. In all his years he'd never received such a generous tip. The smile broadened his face. 'Thank you so very much, Mr...'

'For goodness sake call me Enoch.'

'Sorry, Enoch. Thank you. You must call me when you are ready for your return journey.'

'I don't know when that will be, my friend. But I have your business card. I'll call.'

Raymond stepped forward, greeted Enoch and took his bag.

Enoch entered the house with his head down, sheltering from the rain. He pulled back his black hooded cape from over his face and looked up.

'Buona sera. Good evening.'

Raymond nodded. 'It is so good to see you again, buona sera. Spero tu stai bene?'

'Molto bene, grazie, and you?'

'A little perturbed by all these strange events, but I am well.'

'Do you not remember what I said to you that day?'

Raymond looked blankly at the Italian.

92

'At the lecture, I said that you must never use the words *strange*, or *weird* or *paranormal*. What is *strange* hey? Something that's strange or different to one person, may not be strange or different to another. And listen, my friend, everything that happens on *our side* is paranormal to those on the other. Think about it, Raymond.'

The taxi disappeared into the darkness and Enoch moved further inside to greet the Thorne family.

'Benvenuto a casa nostra, Signor Raphael,' Lyn said, desperately trying to remember some Italian, and getting looks of shock and admiration from her husband and son. She had visualized a traditional Vatican Priest, old, long robes, a collar, clutching a Bible. He wasn't from some movie. This man was dressed in casual black trousers, a white shirt and radiated a friendly persona. 'Prego.'

'Grazie, Signora Thorne.'

Stan ushered Reuben aside to allow some space for the visitor.

'We have a room for you to stay, Mr Raphael. Actually, my son, Reuben has kindly offered up his room for you.'

'Thank you, Reuben.' Enoch shook Reuben's hand and edged into the living room.

'I know it's late, Mr Raphael, but would you care for a drink?' Stan tried hard to impress.

Reuben smiled devilishly at his father. It was all such an act, so false.

Enoch spotted the painting. 'This is the painting, yes?'

The others all nodded.

'And it was painted by Dexter. Dexter Manning. I have foreseen this in a vision. I have seen this painting and I have seen Mr Manning, too. The man who painted

93

this picture is Dexter Manning – he lived at Ivy cottage.'

'How do you know this?' Stan asked.

Enoch did not reply immediately. He thought about the question before answering. 'In my line of work, many things come to me in vision and spirit. And the internet.'

Reuben grinned, but shuffled uncomfortably. 'This is weird. Dexter Manning lived at the old cottage? He was the old man that nobody knew. My God! It's almost as if the painting came home. I mean, he only lived down the road. That is spooky.'

Enoch took a good look, right into the heart of the image. 'Not weird, not spooky, my boy. It is destiny.' He continued to study the images in the painting whilst talking. Then Enoch jolted back suddenly.

'Mr Raphael,' Raymond helped steady him. 'You okay?'

'Yes, my dear boy, I am fine. But that image is very powerful. So very powerful indeed.'

'What do you see?'

'A doorway into another dimension. Pathways to evil. Mr Thorne,' he turned to face Stan. 'Your offer of a drink would be accepted most graciously.'

'Coffee?'

'Actually I would prefer something a little stronger – how do you say in English? Something with a bit of a kick to it?'

Stan smiled. 'Yes that's what we say. Good ole Scottish Whisky?'

'Please.' Enoch shook his head at the painting. 'After seeing what I have just seen inside that image, I really do need this whisky.'

The time was 11:58. Enoch looked around the room and back at Stan. 'Where is your daughter?'

Lyn spoke up. 'She had a fright earlier. She is resting.'

'A fright?' Enoch leant forward. 'What do you mean?'

'She saw things, awful things, in the bathroom. Something about blood in the water and faces in the mirror.'

Enoch nodded. 'This is very common. These are visions implanted in the mind and used by evil spirits. The visions are mostly of your own images – how you perceive evil. Much of it is from Hollywood. The blood-in-the-bath thing, faces in mirrors, writing on walls, heads turning, chilling figures sitting in chairs. These are already in our minds and are used by evil spirits.'

Stan nodded. This man made sense. But maybe they did collectively imagine that scary figure, Stan wondered. Could he have knocked over the chair in panic? It felt as if he were battling against his own mind. 'So, evil spirits use pre-existing pictures that are stored in our data banks. So they use our own mind against us.'

'Exactly, my friend. Now, it is almost midnight. I have arrived in good time, but now I must do something. In just over one minute we crossover to an important date. Tomorrow holds a link to many events. Dexter Manning and the number thirteen are one and the same.'

Stan threw him a look that meant 'I have no idea what you are talking about.'

Enoch looked at each person. 'The dead can be very useful sometimes. I am going to pray for Dexter Manning, then at the stroke of midnight, I will speak to him to find out what is going on.'

There was silence.

95

Then Enoch knelt down and began to pray, almost in a chanting fashion.

'Dexter Manning. Surge a Purgatorio. Ut forma. Dei expectat.'

They waited. The clock struck twelve. Then they heard a heavy ticking – the ticking of an old grandfather clock. Then they heard a voice.

Footsteps were heard, slow, cautious footsteps coming down the stairs. Lyn gripped Stan's hand firmly. The hairs on the back of her neck stood on end. Her chest tightened and her breathing became shallow.

The door creaked open slowly.

Another voice was heard. It was a mixture of an old man and a young woman.

# Chapter Thirteen

## Friday Thirteenth

'Melissa?' Lyn whispered.

It was one of the most haunting things that Enoch had ever witnessed. It was *the* most haunting thing for the others, yet far more would come.

Melissa entered. Her eyes were as wide as saucers and bloodshot. Her face was pale, almost hinting on a grey tone in the dim lighting of the living room. She spoke.

'I am Dexter Manning. Do not fear me. I live in your world and mine. I cannot leave for…'

'No!' Lyn yelled. 'Melissa!'

Enoch threw Lyn a scowl. The silence had been broken, the link severed. Dexter Manning disappeared from within his host. Melissa collapsed to the floor. Reuben lurched off the armchair and grabbed his sister.

'Melissa,' he called. 'Help me with her,' he demanded.

Raymond moved over and helped Reuben raise her and place her into the armchair.

Both Lyn and Stan were too frightened to move.

Enoch stood up. 'It is with pity that the link was broken. Lyn, you should not have called for your daughter. She would have been all right – Manning was only using her as a means to talk.'

'But why her?' Stan asked.

'Because she was in a vulnerable, weak state of mind – the shock of earlier that you speak about had left her soul fragile. She was the easiest host.'

'Host?' Stan yelled. 'She is our daughter – not a host

for summoning up the dead.'

'Please,' Raymond looked across at Stan. 'Mr Thorne, Melissa is fine.'

'That's all right for you to say, young man. I want you and your friend to stop messing with our lives, stop using us like some kind of experiment. In fact, I want you out of my house.'

'Please, Mr Thorne, we are trying to help.'

'Help? You've got some funny idea of the word help.'

'Melissa is all right.'

'What would you care if anything happened to her anyway?'

Raymond looked into Stan's eyes and then into Melissa's. 'I care a lot, Mr Thorne.'

Stan felt his insides boil.

'Stan, please.' Lyn held his hand and gave him a passive look. 'Not now. Let's all just get some rest. Raymond and Enoch will stay here. Now, let's just get some rest, all of you.'

A good sleep was had by all. Stan had previously decided to go into work late; after all, he'd worked hard without a day off sick or holiday for several months so he rewarded himself with a nice lay-in.

Lyn advised the kids to stay home. She would make a phone call to the school head teacher and explain that there were serious family issues that prevented both Melissa and Reuben from attending. Lyn knew that she could not tell the truth. Who on earth would believe her? Or, she then thought, who on the earth that we once knew? She had started to question everything that she said and did. She felt paranoia build up inside, and she had no idea what was really going on.

'Buongiorno,' Enoch said, stretching.

Lyn turned away from the cooker. 'Oh, Mr Raphael, did I wake you?'

'No, no. I was awake, but my eyes would not open. I am surprised that I slept so well.'

'It seems that we all did. This must be the best night's sleep we've had in days.'

Enoch looked past her and onto the cooker. 'What are you cooking?'

'Oh, nothing. I don't really know why I am standing here.'

Enoch noticed an open utensil draw, three pots on the cooker and yet, no food.

'Melissa, Reuben...' Lyn called. 'Breakfast.' She looked at the Italian. He was unshaven, had a balding scalp and sort of hollow eyes. Enoch was quit tall and slim. Then she remembered something. Her blood almost turned cold, her heart skipped a beat. She saw that awful vision again – the one she had on Monday when she looked into the painting.

Enoch laughed quietly and wickedly like a comic book super-villain. 'I am sorry,' he said, still smiling. 'You see the vision again, don't you?'

Lyn nodded.

'Do not worry. That vision will never become a reality.'

'But...' Lyn felt her voice quiver. '...you were in that vision – you were the evil priest that was about to sacrifice my dog.'

Enoch shook his head. 'My dear, yes, it was I in that vision but the dog was all in your mind.'

'I don't follow.'

'I saw that vision at the same time that you saw it. But my version was slightly different. In my version, you were standing inside the church, at the door, smiling at me. I was holding a knife, ready to slice some fruit. There was no dog, no sacrifice in my vision.'

'So, why did my mind make the vision so evil?'

'Because your mind has been poisoned. All of you, in fact, nearly everyone on this planet. Your minds have been shaped and moulded by society – all the bad things that you witness, everything you see on the news, all that you hear – it's all so bad and so evil that the subconscious part of the human brain can only think in negative means.'

Stan had been leaning against the kitchen door unnoticed. 'If I may come in on this conversation?'

Enoch spun his head and smiled at Stan. 'Of course. What is it that you wish to share?'

'It's not so much what I have to share, it's more of a question.'

Enoch nodded for Stan to continue.

'You talk of negativity in the brain as a cause of these awful visions. Okay, but why do *you* not see such terror?'

'Ah, that is a riddle in itself; an all-time tricky puzzle. But I believe that I know the answer.'

Enoch checked the faces of his listeners. Melissa, Reuben and Raymond had arrived and had begun to listen. They all had the same expression of intrigue.

'I do not only see the wicked one in my visions, I also see the pure. To the pure and clean conscience, all things are equal. You see, I am a servant of God and rarely go by the ways of the modern world.'

Melissa entered the kitchen and sat down. The others followed suit. Lyn poured coffee into six mugs and then sat herself down.

'Enoch,' Lyn did not make eye contact. She did not need to see another vision. 'Are you saying that we are all sinners and do not have a clean conscience?'

Enoch caught Raymond's eye. 'Would you like to field this question, Raymond?'

Raymond cleared his throat. 'I believe that we are all sinners. It is widely spoken through every religion – the word sinful is often misused. It simply means that we are all imperfect, ever since man turned away from God, having been given freewill. Since the times of Genesis, we all know the story of Adam and Eve – they sinned against God and belief has it that every human from that moment on has been born with impure form, or sin.' Raymond looked at Melissa who was sat close to him. 'This is just one reason we, as mankind, look at all life in negative fashion.'

Stan and Lyn shifted their gaze to Melissa.

'What?' Melissa said, clasping both hands tightly together on the table. 'I was really freaked out in the bathroom. I know you all think I'm crazy…'

'No,' Stan hurled the word at Melissa like a cricket ball into her face. 'Nobody thinks you are crazy. We've all had horrible visions – look what happened to your mother – the writing on the wall? We are all in this together and none of us are crazy. If what Enoch and Raymond say is true, then there is only one way we can solve this – by sticking together.'

'You are indeed a wise man, Stan,' Enoch declared. 'We will work through this mystery of intrigue and nightmares. But…' he paused. 'Raymond, as a one-time student of mine, maybe you can complete your hypothesis about the sinning of mankind? Maybe you could tell everyone about the wicked one?'

All eyes were glued on the young man's face. Raymond dropped his eyes to the table. This was the first time he had given a lecture, and he was rather nervous. 'As I said, we are all sinners and we emit a strong negative energy. Those who have turned to God, repented their sins and choose a pure life – I mean moved away from bad things – have a clean conscience and pure heart. They emit a positive energy. But, as many believe in the scriptures from Genesis to Revelation, there's a far greater evil power that has corrupted all mankind. Those pure and faithful servants of God cannot be touched by him.'

Stan nodded as he remembered his studies from many years ago. 'Satan has corrupted mankind and there are thousands of fallen angels that work for him.' He scanned around the table and noticed some surprised reactions. 'What?'

'Nothing,' Lyn said. 'You are truly a wealth of knowledge.'

Melissa had said very little. Her mind was awash with so many thoughts that it flooded her consciousness. Eventually, she managed to piece everything together and revealed; 'Do you remember when I spoke to you about the human brain the other day?' They nodded in response. 'Well, if you recall, the brain has neurotransmitters such as serotonin, yeah?'

Melissa felt like a school teacher talking to class of dumb students. 'Lack of serotonin can...you listening?'

Stan grinned. 'We're taking it all in. Although I'm not sure where this is going.'

'Just listen. Right,' she continued. 'Now, lack of serotonin can lead to problems. Antidepressant drugs help this by balancing the levels of neurotransmitters. Also, some drugs reduce the number of pain signals that get to the brain.' Melissa looked at her father for a response.

'Less pain signals means happier feelings, am I right?'

'What has this got to do with us?' Lyn asked.

'I can see where Melissa is coming from with this,'

Raymond said. 'An imbalance of brain signals leads to negativity. With this, we lend ourselves open to negative thought, negative vision and evil spirits.' He looked at Enoch. 'Just as you said – we don't have pure mind. But it's all of us, not necessarily to do with personal chemical imbalance, it's already there, in our human DNA. We are naturally weak. And that's how the evil spirits, or demons if you like, are getting to us.'

'Evil spirit?' Reuben asked. 'Is this Satan?'

'Yes, my boy,' Enoch said. 'Or at least, as your father stated, others that work for him.'

'Satan?' Lyn quizzed. 'Can this be true, I mean, I never believed in any of this stuff. Satan, really?'

'Yes, Lyn. I think that he, or one of his followers, or more, may be coming through a portal that Dexter Manning has created. A portal that is in the painting.'

'Wow, this is deep,' Reuben said. 'Can't wait to tell the guys at school.'

'Do not inform anyone,' Enoch stood up, aggressively. 'You must not speak to a single soul if you value your life. Understand?'

Reuben gulped down some coffee hard. He nodded, feeling like a timid schoolboy facing a ticking off. 'If we are all basically depressed souls then what do you advise us to do to keep out the devil – endless supply of antidepressants?'

# Chapter Fourteen

## The Book

Stan apologised to his work colleagues for being late. He didn't actually have to, being the supervisor, still, it was pure courtesy. He closed the outside door to the mill and sauntered into his office. He spoke no words regarding the previous phenomenon that had struck his family; it would be better that nobody else knew. That was one reason for keeping Melissa and Reuben at home, under lock and key – the teenagers could not keep their mouths zipped up – especially when something so unusual was taking place.

Stan sat down in his chair and begun to go through the week's accounts, which was to be done every Friday, without fail. It was a regular and time-consuming task, yet, not a difficult one. Stan administered the accounts for both the mill and the printers. He would leave the two boys to run the mill, and Terry Hatchet to run the print.

The week had seen;

1 order of 8 by 5 advertising flyers for Mr Smith of the High Street Charity Shop.

1 order of 8 by 5 advertising flyers for Trevor Jay Plumber and sons.

A set of 200 business cards for Trevor Jay Plumber and sons.

3 window ads of A6 size for the local Scout troop and a further 3 ads of A4 for the same.

5 days' supply of 100 local newspapers for the

Hamden Daily Press.

He stopped, checked the order again and gasped. He turned to see where the boys were – busy running the mill. Good, at least he could fathom out this latest conundrum in peace and quiet.

There was another order; a one-off copy for a book. It wasn't uncommon to take order for a print-on-demand book. Many self-publishers had come through Hamden Print, but there was a process that had to be followed. Firstly, he would check the material for Terry, then, he would recommend a paper quality for the publisher, or author. The written document would be downloaded onto his system, checked again, and then sent over to Terry, who, in turn, would set up the presses and print the desired publication. He would then have one of his guys to set the book, bind it and run through a detailed checking process.

This book had not seen any of this, but according to the computer, it had already been printed.

Stan checked the details again. The customer name was a D.M Journals. Stan shook his head.

'What on earth is this?' he whispered to himself. 'D – M – Journals? Who is it?' He looked about the office for inspiration. Alongside the name of the customer sat the name of the book and the quantity. Only one book, fair enough, he thought. Normally a self-published book would be printed as a one-off first – the proof copy. Nothing unusual there. Stan decided to pop round to the printers to see if Terry knew anything about it.

'Hi, Terry, got a moment?'

Terry nodded. 'Two minutes, Stan. I'll just finish prepping the ink duct rollers, then I'll be with you.'

Stan waited patiently. He began to tap his fingers on an unused image carrier. The drumming of finger on aluminium had begun to irritate one of the young printers.

'Is it anything I can help you with, Mr Thorne?'

'No, it's just something I need to discuss with Terry. Not to worry, I'll come back in a while.'

'It's all right, Stan, hold your horses.'

Terry grinned at Stan, finished the setting up procedure and moved over to the sink. Whilst washing his hands he spoke; 'What is it? You look like you've seen a ghost, Stan.'

'I may have, Terry. I just may have.'

'What are you blathering on about now? I tell you, this week you've not been yourself.'

'Listen, Terry. I've had an order go through the books for a one-off print – a single copy of a book under the name of D M Journals. I haven't seen anything of this – no pre-order, no preparation, no nothing. Do you know anything about it?'

Terry scratched his head like Charlie Chaplin. 'No idea. Nobody can run the print without me knowing and of course, you are the one who develops the correct paper. What is the name of the book?'

'You'd better come over to my office in the mill.'

Terry followed Stan over. They entered the mill and saw the two lads busy at work.

'This is odd,' Stan remarked. 'My documents have moved.' He shifted his ledger and found something underneath. It was a paperback book.

'What the…' he glanced at Terry. 'This wasn't here just now – and before you say anything I am not going crazy.'

Terry put his hands up and said, 'I wouldn't dream of saying anything of the sort.' He smiled, but the smile faded quickly when he saw Stan's face. 'What is it?'

'I think I need a drink.' He passed the book to Terry.

Terry glanced at the cover and flicked through the pages. He turned to the printer details. It had been printed by a different printer. He watched Stan settle slowly into his chair, lower his head onto his hands and sigh.

'This hasn't been printed here, Stan. So, how did the order go through our books?'

Stan shook his head. 'Don't know.'

Terry flicked through the pages again. He read a few random lines. He noticed some very familiar names. 'What? Why…is your name in here?'

'Let me see,' Stan snatched the book away. He frantically scanned random pages. He slammed the book shut with both hands. 'We are all in here – you and I, my family, everyone.'

'So who wrote it?'

'I have an incline. Terry, this is difficult to explain, let's just say it's a story in itself.'

'What?'

'I mean, um…' Stan began to fumble. His words failed to materialise. '…the book, it's…'

'What about the book, Stan?'

'The book is us – we *are* the book.'

'You aren't making sense. Maybe you need some time off – we can use the agency again to…'

'No!' Stan slammed the book down onto the desk. He studied the front cover. It had a picture of a church, its winding pathway leading the eye to the door. Barren trees stood patiently alongside and the sky was dull, with mystical swirls of cloud. The image was unnerving.

Terry leant over the desk and nodded towards the book. 'Do you recognize the book?'

'Yes. Well, I recognize the picture – it is a spitting image of the picture we bought.'

'Ah, yes, the one you told me about. Bought at the charity shop auction, wasn't it?'

'I told you about it?'

'On Monday, you mentioned something about the girls persuading you to bid for a picture.'

'Oh.'

'Anyway, whoever wrote this is mighty cunning – writing about us and then dropping us a copy when we're not looking. Do you know this D M Journals?'

'It's just D M. They are the initials. The name is Dexter Manning.'

Terry frowned. 'The name's familiar. Why do I know that name?'

Stan did not answer.

'So you know this Dexter Manning?'

'Not exactly. But he knows us.'

'I guess he does,' Terry paused and picked up the book, held it lightly on his left palm and pointed at the cover. 'Dexter Manning,' he said sympathetically, 'Is dead.'

Stan nodded.

'I remember reading his obituary in the print.' Terry pursed his lips, frowned and then made a proclamation. 'If he's dead, how did he write this?' Stan made no comment. Terry continued; 'And something I spotted just now when I flicked through the pages – a date – Friday the thirteenth. Stan, that's today.'

'I know. Listen, Terry, you had better go back to the press. I'll get to the bottom of this.'

'Yeah, find out who is messing around.'

'I will,' Stan replied, dishonestly, knowing full well that he already knew who was behind it.

'Oh,' Terry was about to leave when he asked another poignant question. 'The title of the book – does it mean anything to you?'

Stan nodded. 'Yes, yes it does.'

'Mmm,' Terry began to walk out of the office and along the short wooden walkway. 'Interesting.'

'Interesting indeed,' Stan whispered to himself, or at least, he thought that he whispered to *himself*. He never knew if anyone else was around these days. And then the answer came in the form of a light breeze that ruffled the papers on the desk. Stan slammed his hand down onto the lose documents to stop them flying away. He felt a chill like none other. It was ghostly, yet, not as chilling as the title of the book. He studied the cover again. So very clever, he thought. Dexter Manning you cunning old man – you cunning *dead* old man. Stan picked up the book again and held it with both hands and nodded. The story was about *them*; all of them. And as he scanned the early chapters, he smiled. It was all there – the charity auction, Raymond, Enoch, even a bit about some police officers that he'd never heard of. Stan suddenly had a brainwave. What if he read on? Would the book see his future? Or would the words change when the real events caught up to the point where he had read to? Now his brain started to burn with an overtime of heavy questions. Complex situations bombarded his mind. Every paradox under the sun clouded his thoughts.

'Oh boy this is deep,' he groaned. 'If this book is about us, then our future has been foretold – our destiny. If I read on, will I damage the future? Could I change the future? And why am I talking to myself?'

Stan closed the book and studied the work of art on the front – it was an exact copy, albeit in black and white, of the picture that Dexter had painted.

He read the book title out loud:

'The Painting.'

# Chapter Fifteen

## Revelations

Enoch and Raymond were busy at work, trying to decipher the strange writing that Lyn wrote on the wall.

'It's a jumbled mess of Latin words with our names in it,' stated Raymond.

'You don't say,' Enoch replied sarcastically.

'Can you translate?'

'Of course. Raymond, do you know what this means?'

Raymond nodded. He had studied some Latin whilst at the parapsychology course. Yet, this was an ancient, archaic, almost biblical form.

'It says something about sacrifice or enslaved...' Raymond pointed at one word. 'The devil. I don't know these other names.'

Lyn was perched on the edge of the bed uncomfortably. 'I knew what the words meant when I first saw them. How did I know? I never learnt a word of Latin in my life.'

'Lyn,' Enoch spoke softly. 'This is because you have been, for want of a better word – possessed. Someone or something had temporarily become at one with your mind and soul. When this happens, the host is unaware. Do you remember what happened to Melissa last night?'

'Of course I do. Do you think that I would forget *that*?'

'When she walked into the room and spoke in demonic ways, she had the spirit of Dexter Manning inside her. This was a possession. She was weak in the mind – the easiest host for him. But why is he trying to communicate? I don't know.'

Lyn allowed her eyes to wander across the writing, without focusing on any particular word. 'I can see a pattern,' she said. Lyn stood up slowly and then moved closer to the wall dividing the two men. 'Our names – are formed in a circle. There are five names. What does this mean?'

'Well…'

Enoch and Raymond both began to speak simultaneously. 'Sorry,' Raymond apologized. 'Please, Mr Raphael, do continue.'

'Thank you. I guess Raymond has the same reasoning as myself. The five names in a circle? No, not a circle – a star. I have seen this method of communication before.'

'Communication?' Lyn queried.

'Yes, most of the time, the dead cannot talk to us as we would talk to one another. They can communicate via a possessed host such as you had with the writing. Why it is in Latin I do not know, but maybe it's because of the ancient sacrificial language.'

'That still doesn't explain the star thing,' Lyn added.

'If I may?' Raymond asked.

'Of course, Raymond,' Enoch nodded.

'The five-pointed star is a very common ideogram with many uses – but to the Satanist movement it is very important. The five points represent the number five – a mystical and magical number throughout the ages. It is one of the two most important numbers in life.'

'The other number being *thirteen*?' The voice came from the doorway.

Lyn, Enoch and Raymond turned to face the twins.

112

Melissa and Reuben had been listening silently for several minutes.

Reuben spoke again. 'Thirteen, am I right?'

'Yes,' Raymond replied, glancing up at Enoch for clarification. There was a single nod of the head.

'Five and thirteen. The number **thirteen** has various roots with many superstitious meanings. The number *five* has its importance within each and every one of us.' Raymond looked around for a response.

Melissa thought hard for an example. She found a couple. 'Five fingers, five toes.'

'Five wounds of Christ,' added Raymond.

'Five senses of the human body,' Lyn stated.

'I know another one,' Reuben said quietly. 'The famous five?' He instantly felt four sets of eyes burning into him. 'All right, I don't know.'

'That's okay,' Enoch laughed. He moved over to Reuben and placed his hand on his shoulder. 'But you do see that five is important?'

'Yeah.'

'Five elements of the universe.' Raymond grinned. 'I bet you didn't see that one, hey?'

'He's correct,' said Enoch. 'What are the elements Melissa?'

Melissa was caught on the spot. She felt as if she was back in school, in her least favourite subject. 'Um, five elements?'

The Italian nodded at her.

'Well – **earth**, **air**, **water**…and um, I can't remember.'

'**Fire**,' Lyn added.

'Well done. But what is the fifth element?'

Raymond grinned. 'I'll answer this one. The fifth element is **Aether** – that is the material that fills the void of our universe.'

Enoch nodded. 'It's also known to be called **dark energy** amongst many other names. Of course, scientists have argued over the status for hundreds of years. To many, it's simply a myth. In some religious texts, it's described as the void between life and death. In simple form – the quintessential **spirit**. Now, to some of us, there's another name that describes this place, a name you will know.....'

Enoch paused. He studied Melissa intently.

Melissa looked uneasy; she had an idea about this name, the name of the void. Then her mind drifted. 'I've thought of something. In science the other day we learnt about an element called Boron. The atomic number is....'

Reuben cut in, sharply, 'Don't tell me, *Five*?'

'Yeah. It's part of group thirteen of the table. They say its a mystery.'

'Very good,' Enoch replied, in surprise. 'Boron has remained a mystery. Formed after the Big Bang, not inside stars, but within free space – cosmic radiation within the void. It's the key to the evolution of life on Earth.'

'How can any of this help us?'

'It proves the connection between the numbers of five and thirteen. Boron and Aether are essential for all life and the existence of the universe. Five and thirteen.'

'Yes, but Enoch,' Lyn pointed a finger. 'You are a man of religion, aren't you?'

Enoch nodded.

'Then, surely you don't believe in the Big Bang.'

'Oh, my dear Lyn. Few people understand religion. Fewer understand science. You see, religion and science are one and the same.'

'Hey?'

'God created the Big Bang. Yes, in the Bible, in Genesis, it says that God took six days and he rested on the seventh.'

'Yeah, we all know this bit,' Lyn interrupted.

'All right, but the fact is this – it is not to be interpreted literally. One day in God's eyes is many thousands in ours. The book of Genesis does not suggest six earth days. You see? God created the earth through, what science calls, the Big Bang.'

Reuben laughed. 'Yeah, but who created God?'

'Please, Reuben, do not allow yourself to become trapped in that paradoxical question.'

'Hey? Para-what?'

'Forget it, Reuben,' Lyn said. 'We've drifted off the topic here. Let's get back on track. What the heck does this have to do with all this writing on the wall.'

'Of course, Lyn. You are correct. Let us return to the star. But first one must have knowledge of the history before one understands the meaning.'

Lyn nodded and sighed. 'Simple English all right? Go on.'

'Thank you. God created all Angels to perfection. Many, over time, rebelled, or turned, and they fell from heaven. One of them named himself Satan. God allowed Satan to rule the earth as a test for both Satan himself and mankind. Unfortunately, mankind faltered. Now, Satan is very powerful and has control over every one of us. Other powerful Angels, Archangels, rule over thousands of good, and evil demons. How do we know this?'

Raymond replied. 'Sin.' He shook his head. 'Imperfections, greed, murder, war, jealousy…the list goes on.'

'Indeed, my son.' Enoch nodded. 'These demons can reach into our souls and control us. They can do many

115

things, five thousand times in the blink of an eye, and five thousand people all at once.'

'There's that number five again,' Lyn remarked.

'Yes, many connections, five points of the star leading us into the five elements, and *away* from the Demons.'

Raymond turned his head slowly towards the taller Enoch. He raised his eyes and spoke. 'You mean that the star is *not* of the Devil, but *against* him?'

'That's correct. The pentagram does not, in itself, summon the evil spirits from Satan. In some Paganism and Christian belief it has actually been used as a shield. Remember, Satan has no control over the elements, thus no control over the *pentagon of the elements*.'

'But this is a downward pointing pentagram – the symbol for Satanism.'

Enoch ran his fingers over his stubbly chin. 'No, Raymond. Take a closer look at the way the names are positioned. If you draw a line, diagonally between the names to form a pentagram, you'll see that it's an upward pointing star. Also, there are small symbols of the star near to the writing.'

'Ah, yeah, sorry, Mr Raphael. You're correct. So, this has been written by a spirit who is against Satan?'

Enoch took a deep breath and exhaled slowly. 'I don't know. The words are evil – sacrificing you all – but the form of the names is not. It is as if there are two forces at work, both very powerful and both using Lyn as a way of communication.'

'Yes!' Raymond almost deafened his Italian mentor. 'Sorry, Mr Raphael. But…' he smiled and turned to face the others. 'I know what it is all about. The devil wants to sacrifice us all but another force wants to shield us from evil – using the names in the form of an upward

116

facing star. I believe that the force that is acting against Satan is either a collective positive energy from all of us, or someone completely different – a good spirit that is trying to help us. The question is this – is Dexter Manning the Devil, or is *he* the one who is trying to help us?'

# Chapter Sixteen

## Neighbourhood disturbances

Stan completed his work and checked that the lads had cleaned the machines and then checked the mill wheel mechanisms for the following day. Saturdays were never quiet and the fourteenth was to be no exception. Terry had already received orders for the Hamden Sunday Metro, some new hymn sheets for the church and a batch of pamphlets for a law firm. He was mighty pleased that they had chosen Hamden Print. Maybe the old fashion ways were attracting even the most upmarket solicitors. Terry was smiling when he left the building. Stan was not.

On his way home, Stan could not stop thinking about the book. He tormented himself constantly. He glanced across at the digital display. The time and date stood out prominently; five thirteen, Friday thirteenth. He shook his head and mumbled. 'Stupid superstitions.'

The book rested neatly on the seat beside him.

Stan used the driver-side remote switch to lower the nearside window. The cool air was refreshing. But then, the breeze skirted over the seat, rustling up the pages of the book. He glanced down and spotted page thirteen that had blown open. It revealed a hand-scripted letter that almost spoke out to him. Stan swung the Honda over into a bus stop and pulled up. He couldn't care less if a bus turned up; there were far more pressing matters to concern himself with.

Further pages skipped open – he read out several names. 'Farley, That name rings a bell.' He continued. 'Paula Shelby. William Bonné.' Stan grabbed his mobile phone and dialled home. Lyn answered in five rings.

'Hi, honey, it's me. Could you do me a favour? I won't be long, but I'm swinging by the police station on route home.....' Lyn interrupted him but Stan finished, quickly. 'No, nothing's wrong, it's just, I need to check something out. In the meantime, will you ask one of the kids to do a search on the internet for a book titled...' He stopped. His brain worked hard. 'Second thoughts – forget it, don't worry. I'll see you soon.'

Stan decided that he would investigate the weirdness a little further before worrying the others. And he had decided to read on some more. He skipped the pages, turning them swiftly with a moistened forefinger. It was all there – right up to the point where he had left work on Friday evening and pulled up in the bus lane.

Stan felt a headache coming on. This just didn't seem real; it couldn't possibly be real. Stan grinned and shook his head. 'I'll wake up in a minute. This has to be one of those stupid, crazy dreams.' But his smile faded as the reality of the situation became all too real. Stan kept reading. He was reading about himself *reading about himself* – and that hurt his brain so much he almost fainted; the shear complex and pure paradoxical difficulties. His brain began to succumb to the face of madness.

'How can this be?' he asked himself. 'There are only two logical explanations – one, I am dreaming and two, this is a form of paranormal activity, and three – I have gone insane. OK, that's three logical reasons.'

There was a heavy engine sound accompanied by a deep blast of a horn. Stan shook himself back to reality and looked into the rear-view mirror. A local number five bus had pulled up menacingly close behind. Stan waved an apologetic hand and drove away.

Upon arrival at the Hamden Police station, Stan dared himself to read a little more of the mysterious book. He was on page 120.

He hesitated, glanced outside at the quiet surroundings and then refocused his tired eyes back to the next page. As he tried to read on, his eyes became heavy, his head hurt and his ears rang with a sharp piercing wail. He snapped the book shut. The pain stopped.

'Damn you!' he yelled at the book. 'Stop messing with me.'

Stan reopened the book, but this time, he turned to the end of the book. It was blank. Nothing there.

'Weird,' he muttered. 'Really weird.'

He turned back to 120 and began to laugh, nervously, just as the book was instructing. Then he glanced at the words below the sentence he was reading and looked up. Before the police officer outside the car had chance to speak, Stan answered the question.

'No I'm fine, Officer – there's no problem.'

The Policeman opened his mouth to say something but Stan, again, answered.

'Yes Officer, thanks. I'm actually here to see Inspector Farley.'

But then, as if a punishment for reading ahead in the book, Stan felt another intense pain in his head. The sharp pain began behind his eyes and circled his head twice before easing off. He was now certain; he would not be able to foretell the future by reading on.

'I'm afraid,' said the officer, 'Mr Farley has been called out to a disturbance. I'll leave a message if you like.'

'No, that won't be necessary. A disturbance? Where?'

'I'm sorry but I am not at liberty to…'

'Just tell me where? In fact, I already know this bit of course. Pines Avenue, isn't it?'

Stan grabbed the phone and dialled home. There was no answer. He slammed the car into gear and sped away, unperturbed by his speedy actions outside the offices of the law.

Outside house number five Pines Avenue, several neighbours had gathered. They gossiped in whispered tones, with an occasional customary finger pointing.

Then a faint siren could be heard. The noise grew louder and then stopped abruptly as an unmarked Toyota police car turned into view.

Paula Shelby stepped out first. She closed the car door firmly and waited for Inspector Farley.

'What do you think, Tim?' Paula asked. 'Clear them away or ask a few questions?'

'One thing at a time. Let's just knock on the door first. You should know that most domestic disturbances are easily solved with an apology rather than with the police. It's probably nothing.'

'Seems strange though, doesn't it?'

'What seems strange?'

'Well, Sir, this was where we found Dexter Manning. In fact, there's the cottage back down there.'

'Don't remind me, Paula. That was a spooky day.'

'Spooky?' Paula seemed unnerved at his statement. 'I'd say more like sad.'

Farley knocked on the door. The door opened within seconds.

'Hello, my name is Inspector Farley of Hamden Police, we've had reports of some noise and alleged shouting coming from your house.'

Lyn Thorne looked dumbfounded. She shook her head. 'No, we are all fine. In fact I have visitors – a friend from Italy. Um, my husband is due home any second – would you like to wait?'

'No, I'm sure that won't be necessary, but may we just come in and have a quick look around – just to check.'

'Check what?' Lyn asked.

'Some neighbours have complained about a violent domestic disturbance, Ma'am.'

Lyn chuckled. 'Not here, everything's fine, really.'

The inspector was adamant that he and Paula take a quick look around. Lyn was helpless in preventing the police officers from entering.

Farley spotted the painting that was still resting on the floor. He popped his head 'round the kitchen door and was greeted with polite smiles from Reuben and Melissa. Paula, meanwhile made way upstairs. As she turned onto the landing she spotted two men in a bedroom. They appeared to be decorating.

'Hello,' she said, announcing her presence.

Enoch and Raymond replied cautiously to the police woman. She nodded, let her eyes roam the bedroom wall and turned back downstairs.

'Well, I'm sorry,' Farley apologised to Lyn. 'Sorry to have taken up your time. I'll go and have a word with the neighbours and tell them that there is nothing to concern themselves with. Again, please accept my apologies, Mrs Thorne.'

Lyn shut the door and instantly wondered how he knew her name – after all, he hadn't asked for her name and she had not offered it.

'That was close,' Raymond called out. 'We only just managed to get this writing covered up.'

'Well done guys,' Lyn said. 'Nice work.'

Upon first noticing the police, Raymond and Enoch began frantically covering the wall-writing with some old wallpaper that Reuben had found. They had just finished hanging some strips from the top when Paula arrived.

Stan arrived abruptly. 'Did I just see the police leaving?'

'Apparently some kind of domestic had been reported – thanks to the lovely neighbourhood watch,' Lyn announced. 'We hadn't made any noise. Something must have spooked the neighbours – maybe they are getting visions, too.'

Stan asked for everyone to join him in the kitchen.

'What did you tell the police?'

'Nothing,' Lyn replied. She nodded in the direction of Enoch and Raymond. 'The guys quickly hung some old wallpaper and made it look as if they were decorating. I guess it worked – the police woman didn't see the writing.'

'Paula Shelby. The police woman – her name is Paula. The inspector was a Mr Tim Farley. And there's another – his name is William. I'm sure he'll play a part in this book soon.'

'How do you know, Dad. And what book?' Melissa asked.

'I've read it. Up to the present time.' He threw the book onto the kitchen table. 'It's all in here – everything that has happened to us, and Dexter Manning, since he died.'

'What?' Lyn moved towards the book.

'I know how this must sound and I guess you'll think I'm crazy but, the book is writing itself as we go.'

'Let's turn down the crazy, Dad, come back to reality and talk sense,' Reuben glanced up at his father. 'How can a book be about us?'

'Read it,' Stan replied.

But Enoch was as quick as lightning. 'No,' he

slammed his hand down onto the book. 'You must not read from the book – it may turn up something of an undesired consequence.'

'Will you start talking in normal talk,' Melissa said. 'Basics, please.'

Lyn grinned at her daughter. 'She's right. What do you mean, Enoch?'

'If what Stan describes is correct, then the book may be the work of the devil or some other demon – playing with your minds. It would be safer for me to read it, not you, not yet.'

So the family had decided to leave the book unturned. It would remain on the kitchen table for the night. Enoch filled Stan in with the day's findings and any theories before calling it a night. Friday the thirteenth had been a long day, yet it had proved not to be unlucky for them.

'This is so cool!' Reuben announced with a smile. 'All this stuff is just awesome! Just like something from a horror movie.'

Inspector Farley and Paula Shelby had not driven far. They had pulled up just around the corner. Both of them were wise enough and experienced enough to know that something wasn't right, so had decided to keep a watchful eye on number five, for a few minutes more.

# Chapter Seventeen

## Power of the mind

Saturday morning

'I've said it before and I shall say it again; nothing you see in the movies is real.' Raymond shook his head at Reuben. He cupped the mug of coffee in both hands and inhaled the aroma of fresh Arabica bean.

Stan paused for thought, wondering why the young man had suddenly come out with such a profound statement over a morning mug of coffee. He grinned, donned his light jacket, and picked up his brief case. Before he left for work, he turned again and agreed. 'He's right, just because Hollywood writes this stuff, doesn't mean it's real.'

Enoch sighed, took a deep breath and countered Raymond's statement. 'On the contrary, what you see is exactly what happens in the *mind* of the individual who is watching, or indeed reading. As you follow the story, your mind develops a power of believing that there actually are demons and bad things going on.' He paused and confirmed that everyone was listening. 'But most visualisations such as those found in Hollywood horrors are fictional – demonic spirits don't really go about spewing blood, puke or any other lovely liquid, nor swear profoundly and torture people physically.' He grinned devilishly. 'But in a way some do torture, mentally, over a long period of time. In fact, Satan is torturing us as we speak. Each word we read, each word we speak, Satan teases and torments. Our mind stores up so much negative energy and harmful thoughts – and

125

we are unaware of how dangerous it is. Satan can use this against us – remember? He can bring forth those haunted images of the past – bad memories, lost love ones, terrors and nightmares – all brought forward in a bundle of evil.'

'Like in that old movie – Ghostbusters 2.' Reuben added. 'Good movie.'

Stan grinned at his son. 'I wonder how many pop-culture references we can find? The Shining?'

'Definitely. I know another – Candyman.'

'Stephen King's IT – now there's a classic.'

'The Others – that messes with your head.'

Lyn interrupted, 'Have you two finished?'

Stan began to open the door to leave,'OK, yeah, but if psychological horror and past experiences are ingrained in our minds, what happens next?'

'Then,' Raymond sighed, 'It all comes out in the most disturbing visions, as we've seen. And what's more; when you have a vision or a nightmare, your mind actually believes that it's so real that anything can happen.'

'The power of the mind,' Lyn added.

'Precisely. Visions, thoughts, experiences. It's all just signals to the brain. What's important is how the brain decodes each parcel of information. What if neurons end up in the wrong place? You've only got to reverse a path here, and a receptor there, to completely change everything the brain perceives as reality.'

'Our demons have the capability to interfere with the electrical circuits?'

'Yes. While your senses may not be actively sending signals, the brain thinks otherwise, due to the interrupted pathways. As in a hypnotic, dream-like state, everything is real, including seeing things that aren't there.'

126

'And then our response is the same, as if something *were* actually there.'

'To the brain, it's the same thing. The response is panic, run, fight, or whatever.'

Reuben had been digesting the information, but frowned. 'Excuse me, how did we get onto this debate?'

Stan grinned. 'I'll leave you all to it. I'm off to work.' He kissed his wife goodbye and shut the door.

'Well, Reuben,' Enoch replied. 'This conversation started when *you* told us last night that this was just like a movie – a horror movie.'

'Oh yeah. Now I'm beginning to wish I hadn't said a thing.'

'Why is someone getting into our minds?' Melissa asked.

'Maybe he's already here. Always has been inside one of us,' Reuben answered with a wry smile. 'After all, Dad's name is Stan, that almost spells Satan.'

'That's not funny, Reuben.' Melissa glared at her brother and then glanced at Lyn. 'Mum, tell him to stop being so stupid.'

'Stop it Reuben. Your sister's right. This isn't the time for silliness.'

Lyn turned to Enoch, changing the subject slightly. 'I don't know how you can cope, Enoch, with all the bad spirits and all.'

'I learn to cope. But, yes, it can sometimes be disturbing.'

'Don't you ever get nightmares from your work?'

'I don't mind having bad nightmares because I know that when I wake up reality is far worse.'

Lyn glanced sideways at Melissa. They exchanged puzzled looks. For a moment they were silent.

'Well, that clears that up,' Lyn said.

'Mum.' Melissa moved over to the painting and studied it. 'This painting is the cause of everything weird that is happening. This is controlling our minds, controlling our nightmares. Whoever is in there is watching us every minute of the day.'

Enoch sat down in the dark leather chair. He smoothed his forehead in deep thought. 'The human brain is more powerful than you think – but it is easily fooled as we have discussed, and can overpower your entire senses, shutting down the vital organs as an escape from the nightmarish reality. You see, what starts off as a non-reality can so very quickly turn into one real nasty reality.'

'You literally get scared to death?' Melissa added.

'Exactly. That is how Satan works.'

'But we can fight against him by believing in ourselves, believing in one another and remaining strong?'

'Guys,' Lyn said, 'This is deep.'

Enoch grinned. 'It is very deep. Lyn, all I'm saying is that you must not be fooled by your own mind.'

'Easier said than done.'

'Can I ask something?' Reuben knelt down in front of the painting. He looked into the windows of the church. 'Why is the painting doing this to us?'

'I've said it already; it is not the painting,' Enoch answered. 'It is Dexter Manning. For some reason, his soul – his spirit, is trapped in there. He is reaching out, into our minds. He connects with anyone who shares his history such as relatives, or in your case, a painting that is part of him.'

'That didn't answer my question.'

'Dexter is a lost soul, or a spirit who is trapped between this world and the next. There is much anger with him and this is what is being released.'

'Yeah, so where does Satan fit in?'

'Dexter is either using the powers of Satan to release his anger, or Satan is using Dexter to toy with our minds. Whatever, Dexter is within this void of the damned – the trapped space between life and death.'

Melissa remembered back to yesterday's conversation. 'Aether – the fifth element – that you said filled the void of our universe. I have a feeling there is another name for this place.'

Enoch raised himself up from the chair and placed his hand gently onto Melissa's shoulder. 'You are indeed most intelligent. Melissa, you are a very clever girl.'

'I am?'

Enoch nodded. 'I know what you are thinking. Say it, please. What is this word that describes the void?'

Melissa grinned, unnaturally, looked down at the carpet, and spoke. 'Hell.'

'Hey, hang on, now,' said Lyn. 'Hell?'

Melissa nodded. 'Dexter is in hell.'

'We can help Dexter, and release him from his pain. We can help him get to his chosen path.'

Raymond, who had been standing in the doorway quietly, spoke. 'How?'

Enoch shook his head, slowly. 'I'm uncertain.'

Raymond added, 'And there's a flaw. If we release Dexter from purgatory, or wherever, another soul may have to replace his. The devil will not take too kindly to interference. By giving him a soul back, at least he will be able to continue his work.'

'His work?' Lyn asked.

'Have you ever heard of soul takers?'

'No. Well, maybe, thought it was a movie.'

'It was once a mythical chapter of life, but now, we know that is as real as the living flesh. Exodus 21:24

states an eye for an eye – now, the devil has added something else.'

'A soul for a soul.'

'Precisely.'

'But who's soul should replace Dexter Manning's soul?' Reuben asked.

Enoch nodded. 'A valid question, my son. Indeed, a valid, and unanswerable question. But we must not jump to conclusions. We do not know yet, if a soul is required. And if indeed a soul is given up, it is not I who shall decide. I cannot say whom it is that shall give up there soul to the devil. But the time will come when the chosen one shall be named.'

'If that time comes,' Lyn added sternly.

# Chapter Eighteen

## Soul taker

Giving up their soul to the Devil was not exactly the answer they were looking for. The Thorne family had never even considered the existence of Satan let alone giving up a soul to him. But in light of the past few days, anything seemed possible; and likely.

'Do we draw straws?'

'Don't be silly, Reuben.'

'I'm not.'

Lyn glared at her son. 'Nobody's giving up their soul to anyone, let alone the devil. Anyway, I don't even know why I'm having this crazy conversation because I don't even believe in all this stuff.'

'None of us did, until now, Mum,' Melissa replied.

Lyn turned to Raymond. 'What do you think? Do you have any idea as to how we release Dexter's trapped soul by giving up one of ours? And why on earth should we do that anyway? And what are you still doing here – don't you have a home of your own?'

Raymond began to laugh. 'Oh Mrs Thorne...'

Melissa smiled. 'Mum is just full of questions.'

'Damn right! I have so many questions – and here's another one – why don't we just throw the painting onto a fire and rid us of this curse?'

Raymond looked sternly at Lyn. 'Firstly, if it is a curse, as you say, it cannot be lifted by simply burning the painting. Remember, they are in our minds. By simply burning the painting before we know exactly who we're up against may fuel the anger. Then the Devil, or other demon, will find alternate ways to use

Dexter and get into our minds; if it is the Devil. Secondly, nobody said that we had to give up one of our souls to release Dexter. It's only speculation anyway – I don't know for sure that he's in purgatory and I don't know how we release him if he is. Thirdly, you ask why should bother to release Dexter? Same answer as number one; if we don't help, we may never rest. He may use the Devil to work up some new ways of using us to release him. Or if it's the Devil's own handiwork, then that would be even worse.'

'So it's a no-win situation.'

'At the moment I'm afraid it is.'

'One question left unanswered,' Lyn muttered.

Raymond nodded. 'Yes, I should be getting back to my parent's house. I've spent two nights away and sleeping on the floor isn't as comfortable as you might think.'

'I never thought it was comfortable, Raymond.'

'I'd better get back now, thanks for being so kind and understanding, Mrs Thorne.'

Lyn grinned. 'Didn't think I was.'

Raymond grabbed his belongings and held Melissa's hand with a gentle clasp. 'I'll message you later, but call me if you need anything.'

Melissa nodded. 'Will do.'

Reuben had now sauntered downstairs and into the kitchen, blurry eyed. 'Morning all,' he grunted.

'Morning Reuben. Thanks again Mrs Thorne,' Raymond called. 'Bye, Melissa, Reuben. See you later Enoch.'

As he called up the stairs, Raymond suddenly realised Enoch's unusual absence. 'Hey guys, is he up there?'

'I guess so,' Lyn replied. 'He's probably lying in – he's had little sleep recently.'

'I've got a bad feeling about this.'

'Mr Raphael?' Lyn knocked twice, softly, on the closed door. 'Enoch?'

A few seconds passed and she opened the door, slowly, Enoch was inside. He seemed to be praying. Lyn quietly closed the door, but not fully. She pressed her ear to the small opening between door and frame. Out from the corner of her vision came Stan. Lyn turned and pressed her finger against her lips.

They listened in silence as Enoch spoke, very quietly, in Latin. It was a form of prayer. But something was different, he seemed to be having a one-sided conversation, or one-sided from their perspective.

Lyn pulled the door shut and motioned Stan to return back downstairs with her.

'Who was he talking to?' Stan asked, intrigued.

'No idea, but that's what prayer is, right?'

'Guess so.'

Reuben was munching, noisily on breakfast cereal, slurping milk between mouthfuls. Lyn scowled at him, but left it there. Slurping milk was really not high on the agenda of problems to solve.

'Reuben, we....ah,' Lyn stopped in her tracks, as she heard Enoch walk on the stairs. She turned and moved out from the kitchen to greet the Italian.

'Buongiorno.'

'Good morning to you, Mrs Thorne. Stan, Reuben. Where is Raymond?'

'Oh, you've just missed him but he'll be back later,' Lyn replied.

'Fine. You may have heard me, moments ago, in prayer?'

'You knew, we, um, it was not our intention to evesdrop, Mr Raphael,' Lyn bumbled.

'No problem. I was in morning prayer. But I spoke

of a vision, I asked what this vision was. At night, you see, I saw some more peices of this intriguing puzzle.'

'Go on,' Stan became more than interested, he needed more.

'I was mistaken before when I spoke of the Devil, for it is not his work, not directly. Many demons, spirits and fallen Angels work for him. Our demon, who has been tormenting your souls, who has been at battle with Dexter Manning, is a spirit form, a fallen Angel. I do not yet know of his name. But he is the one. There may be others. Now, Dexter is in a place called Purgatory, or Barzakh, where purification exists, he is being tested.'

Melissa sat quietly, absorbing it all. She nodded.

'Don't you have anything to add, Melissa, you seem to know about this stuff,' Reuben asked.

'Why, what?' She threw Reuben a scowl. 'Why should I know about this?'

'Enough you two, don't start.' Stan was in no mood for the kids to argue. 'Please, Mr Raphael, continue.'

'I'm afraid I have little more, but all that's happened, those awful visions, the possession of Melissa – this was the work of our evil angel.'

'Not a lot to go on, but we are stepping forward. If Dexter truly is a good guy, or whatever, and this demon is bad, what the hell can we do about it?'

Enoch chuckled. 'Oh my son, you must not use the term Hell so loosely. In answer, I need you to have Raymond return, promptly. I have guidance, yet I shall ask for more through prayer.'

Enoch sat in silence, eyes closed, in pure prayer.

# Chapter Nineteen

## Melissa the Angel

It was still early on Sunday morning and Enoch asked everyone to remain calm and quiet, and to do exactly as instructed. He spoke.

'I have foreseen this moment for a very long time, in visions. I had seen many visions, many parts of a puzzle, over so many years. The puzzle is almost complete my friends. Now, I ask of you, to help me.'

'Of course,' Lyn replied.

'Lyn, take this book.'

Lyn slowly received the book from Enoch. She studied the front picture of Hamden Church. 'What should I do?'

'Open the book to this page. You know the page in your mind.'

'I do?'

'Yes, Lyn. Reach for the number.'

Lyn turned to 135. It was *the* page. Seeing the words appear as she read them was most surreal.

'Lyn, turn the page.'

'Ahh!' Her fingers burnt. 'Damn it,' she cried, dropping the book. 'Thanks,' she said sarcastically.

'That is as I expected. In time you will believe in yourself, all of you, and then believe in the good that presides over us. Then, with guidance, you shall read your future, but only as far as the book will allow. Don't forget it's bad luck to read too far ahead in a book. You must never skip a page, nor read the ending before it's time.'

'You keep saying *time*. Time is something we don't

have a lot of, and it's running out.'

'Patience, Lyn. Patience.'

Easier said than done, she thought, patience had run out a long time ago. 'All right, I'll try.'

'Good. When you *can* read ahead, you shall see your destiny. From there, we can fight the demon, change the course of time, change our future.'

'Hang on a minute,' Reuben came in. He looked across the kitchen table at Raymond. 'You can't change the future just as you can't change the past. How can a future that's already written, be written if you change it?'

'Wow! Well put, Reuben,' Raymond exclaimed, 'Actually, you're right, to some extent.'

'Go on.'

'Every event has a result. Causality. Every action follows another action caused directly as a result of the previous. And so on. If you change your mind, change a decision, you change causality, this is determinism. The previously determined outcome is changed, so you change the future.'

'Like going to make a coffee and deciding to make tea instead?'

'Absolutely. There are billions of examples. But you understand; changing the past is, well, not so easy.'

'You got that right,' Reuben grinned. 'There's a lot I'd change. Like punching Kyle in the face and asking Jennifer to the prom before he could.'

Melissa pulled a face. 'You're unbelievable, and who's Jennifer?'

Enoch grinned. 'My son, you are young and there are few moments of your past worth regretting. Your future is what you must work towards.'

Lyn glanced across at Enoch. 'Back to the future, not the movie, but what you made me do just now – burn my fingers on the book.'

'Pop-culture reference,' Reuben added.

Lyn ignored him and continued to face Enoch. 'Um, this is weird, but I feel as if this moment has already taken place.'

'I'll field this one,' Raymond said. 'Lyn, have you ever had a déjà vu?'

Lyn nodded.

'For unknown reasons, we sometimes skip or shift in the space-time continuum, maybe leap forward a bit. You might see, say a cat. It's really nanoseconds and you return to current time. You see the cat, and that's why you have a feeling that you've seen the moment before – déjà vu. Just now, the book – you probably did glimpse the future but just a glimpse, that's all.'

'So with effort, I could see more?'

Raymond shrugged his shoulders.

'Reuben, maybe you could try the book?' Enoch asked.

'No way, I ain't opening that thing.'

'I'll do it,' Melissa stated. 'Don't forget,' she threw Enoch a look of disparity. 'I'm weak.'

'I meant nothing in calling you weak, Melissa. It was just....'

'I get it, duh.' Melissa glanced around at everyone then took the book. 'I was weak when the demon entered, but now I can use that weakness to allow him back inside my head, and we can work out a way to end this.'

Stan took a moment to realise the situation – his daughter, had suddenly grown up. She was no longer a childish teen fighting in the back of the car, sulking, bitching. She was a mature young woman, making tough decisions. A tear formed in his eye. He took his eyes off Melissa and looked at Enoch.

'Is this dangerous?' he asked.

'This gateway through your mind, to the demon, can be opened, but you must understand that if it cannot be closed, you will not return.'

'Oh no, no, no, no. No way.' Stan wagged a finger at Enoch. 'She's not risking losing her mind. Literally.'

'It is your choice, Melissa. It will be your burden to bear.' Enoch looked straight into her eyes. 'It is for you to decide your own future.'

Reuben, in a condescending tone, piped up. 'Enoch will you stop talking Tolkien for a minute. Everything you say seems like it's from Lord of the Rings.'

'Reuben,' Lyn cautioned. 'Enoch is here to help and talks better English than you.'

'Speaks. Mum, you just said *talks better*, and you tell me that my English is bad?'

'Oh knock it off you two,' Stan said firmly. 'Can we allow Melissa and Enoch to work this out?'

'It's okay Dad. I've made up my mind. Let's go to the living room, more space.'

Sitting on the living room floor, she slowly opened the book and turned straight to the current page, that was speaking out to her, every single motion, every word, there for her to see. Melissa began to read, slowly and precisely: *'Melissa began to read, slowly and precisely, working her way through the words....'*

'Yeah,' Reuben cut in. 'We know this bit. Just read the future parts, moron.'

'Reuben quiet!' Enoch's voice was sharp and his facial features stern. 'Continue, my child.'

Reading on, she felt burning in her fingers. Turning the page, she saw nothing.

A quake inside her body, a searing pain in her eyes, her head hurt as if hit by a hammer.

Jasper sat bolt upright as if he'd heard a voice in the hallway. He studied the space intently, he knew that someone had called him. Someone had told him to go to his bed. He could see that 'someone' as a ghostly apparition and they were a trusted friend. Jasper scampered upstairs.

Melissa screamed.

Calmness followed. It was beautiful. She felt herself walking through cool water, waves lapping over her feet, footprints left behind were washed away by the next swoosh of sea. A cool breeze flowed around her, calming. Beautiful.

A man, an elderly man, stood on the beach.

'Are you Dexter?'

'Yes, Melissa, you are my saviour.'

'Take my hand Dexter. Walk with me.'

Tears rolled down Lyn's cheek and Stan gripped her hand. Watching their loving daughter enter a virtual reality into a different realm was one of the toughest things they had witnessed. They needed one another so much right then. Their hands gripped tighter. They saw Melissa's eyes; hollow and dark, her pupils dilated, like black saucers. Her skin was pale.

The energy in the house increased, a power, good and evil, washed over the room. There was a cool breeze. Everyone could hear the sound of the sea. They all listened, hardly breathing, just listening.

'Melissa, you are my good angel. I will tell you my story. When I died, I died unhappy. I allowed Angels to befriend me, I was in a dark place, not heaven, not hell. Some place in between. They promised me so much happiness for all eternity, they would teach me the arts, the power of the stars, guide my every step. They were my friends.'

'What happened, Dexter. What did they do?'

'Melissa, and those with you who listen to my every word. Enoch Raphael, you must help me as I wish to help you. These Angels, fallen from heaven many millennia ago are tricksters, devourer of souls. I can not leave this place of purgatory and all I want is peace. The demon Angels, these tricksters, the names are...'

'Ahhh!' Melissa cried out in pain, falling sideways.

Lyn flung herself forward towards her. 'Melissa!'

Stan rushed over. 'Let's sit her up. Help us Reuben.'

Having positioned Melissa carefully in the soft armchair, Stan turned to Enoch. 'For Christ's sake do something.' He felt like grabbing the man by his collar, but refrained.

Enoch stared at the girl. Her eyes were still wide open like saucers, gazing lifelessly into oblivion, skin pale. He said nothing.

'Jesus! She's not breathing.' Stan felt an increase of terrified emotion, tears formed.

Reuben pushed his parents away. 'Raymond, come here and help. She's not breathing, we have to resuscitate. Do you know how?'

In shock, Raymond moved over. 'No, I, I..'

'I just learnt this at summer camp, do exactly what I say.'

Raymond, eyes full of tears, nodded.

'Help me lower her to the floor. Ready, lift.'

With Melissa lying on the floor they began.

'One, two three....'

'Breath into her Raymond, twice, big breaths.'

After several minutes the young men were exhausted, but battled on.

They stopped.

Reuben collapsed over her and hugged her tighter

than ever before, his emotions let go and he burst into tears.

Lyn collapsed to the floor and Stan, in floods of tears grabbed her. Through the tears he could smell burning. He managed to make eye contact with Raymond, who could smell it also.

Raymond nodded and brushed past Enoch who was standing, almost dormant near the door.

The Painting was burning. The church smouldered away. Raymond grabbed it and felt the heat. It was real, he knew it, this was no vision. He placed it outside, propped up against the wall. Raymond heard Stan call out to him.

'Let the damn thing burn. Let it burn.'

Raymond rushed back in. 'Enoch, please help. What shall we do?'

'Do not fear.' Finally Enoch spoke, but stood remarkably still. 'It is done.'

'What? What is done. Talk to me.'

'They are here.'

'Who?' But then Raymond heard a large vehicle pull up. He moved to the front doorway.

Jasper had remained unusually quiet, waiting for his moment; he rushed back down, out through the open door and greeted two paramedics. The dog, tail wagging, barked twice and rushed back to the door, turned and barked again. He scampered into the living room, licked the face of Melissa and ran back upstairs.

'Complete with kit, the paramedics, a man and a woman were greeted by Raymond.

'Where is she?' asked the female paramedic.

'Through here.' Raymond had an idea who had called them, whether he believed in miracles or not didn't matter right then.

Stan looked bemused. Nobody had called for an

ambulance. And WHY had nobody called for an ambulance?

The paramedics took note of the situation. They had spotted a smouldering painting on the way in, yet nothing else seemed out of place. 'Is this Melissa?' the male paramedic asked.

'Yes, I'm her father.' Stan asked, 'How do you know her name?'

'We were close by and, I, I don't know.' The female paramedic glanced at Enoch whilst beginning to work on Melissa. 'You Mr Raphael? The one who spoke to me? How did I know?'

'I did speak to you. Thank you for coming.'

The paramedic looked at him in disbelief, yet then in complete understanding. She knelt down alongside her colleague and they began. 'All clear, one, two, three.'

Raymond nodded at Enoch. He knew exactly what he had done. His mentor had produced a miracle. He was now a true believer.

Stan also looked at the Italian, with appreciation. 'How?'

'Stan, you called out for Jesus Christ didn't you?'

Stan looked sheepishly down at the floor.

'I meant nothing in it, I ...'

'He heard you.'

'Hey?'

'You called, he came. I asked for his guidance and spoke to the paramedic here.'

After four minutes the male paramedic stopped, removed the defibrillator away, shook his head once and sighed, time ten forty-four am. His colleague bit her lip and glanced up at Lyn.

'No,' Lyn croaked, 'No, no.'

# Chapter Twenty

## Fallen Angels

Enoch stood bolt upright.

'Quia caritas dei nostri Jesu Christi, pura Angelus vitae dat fortitudinem, dat ei vitam significatione, huic puero dat vitam ut et ipsa possit esse in pura lux.'

'Pura Lux.'

A flash of bright, almost blinding light lit up the room. Melissa's lifeless body jumped.

'Again!' screamed the female paramedic. 'Defib once.....one, two three, clear!'

Melissa jumped. They began basic resuscitation again and Melissa coughed, she coughed again, her body twitched. 'Roll her. Check her airway. Pulse. Good. One,....two. Pulse slow. Lifepak EEG on.'

Everyone waited with baited breath. Silence.

'She'll be OK. How?' The paramedic looked at Enoch. In all her years she had never witnessed anything like it. A mysterious voice in her head, urging her to call in a response, that according to the call-handlers, did not exist. She knew the address and urged her colleague to drive, fast. Upon arrival, the living room was exactly as she had 'seen.' She even knew the name of the patient. And now, as they were to announce the time of death. A miracle. That was all she could call it. A miracle.

'You did this?' she stated, still looking at Enoch with admiration.

'Not I alone, all of us. You saved her with us all. A

143

collective power is far greater than the power of one. You are caring people. We are all of caring nature. With our combined power, Melissa lives.'

It was a most surreal, wonderful moment for Lyn, when Melissa looked into her eyes; eyes that were no longer hollow black, but the pale blue loving eyes that she knew. Lyn held Melissa tightly.

'Mum,' Melissa coughed again. 'You're squeezing me.'

Reuben wiped his eyes. 'Glad to have you back sis.'

Easing Melissa into the chair, the male paramedic demanded that she be taken to hospital for further checks.

'I'm fine. Really. Thank you.'

'You'll need to sign this disclaimer. But I still would prefer it if you take her in today.'

Stan nodded. 'We will. Thanks so much for saving her, please, your names?'

'This is Ellie, I'm Ron.'

'Thanks again.'

Enoch held out his hand to Ellie. She took it, expecting a quick hand shake. But she saw a flash of visions. There were two men, one looked like a clergyman, they were coughing. There was smoke. Flames. She blinked and pulled her hand away. 'What was that?' she asked Enoch.

'My dear, I think you know.'

'We've gotta go Ron. The church is on fire. Call it in.'

The ambulance sped away, blues on, siren blaring.


Melissa sat quietly, nestled within her mother's arms. Fragments of information ran through her mind like tiny pieces of a puzzle, all needing to be put together. She knew what was needed. 'Mum, I've gotta finish this. I need to go back.'

'No you don't. Listen, you...'

'Mum, listen. I must help Dexter, who can help us. I have no choice. He is still in battle with the demons.'

'Melissa,' Stan stood tall over her. 'Your mother's right. You aren't going back, it's too dangerous.'

'I've made my choice. I can remember so much, but I need to put it in order.'

'What do you remember?' Raymond asked.

'I remember seeing flashes of images, weird stuff, just after Dexter was taken. He was with me on a beach, it was called Paradise. I remember, the demon that took him, his name was Lucifer.'

'What?'

'Lucifer.'

'Yeah,' Raymond raised his eyebrows. 'I mean, *the* Lucifer?'

Melissa nodded again. 'But there's more. Another demon, angel, or something. And two more, no, four strange demon things, not people, not anything, I mean, nothing like our common visions of what they look like.'

'Four? Who were the others?'

'I don't remember.' Melissa held her head, it was pounding.

'Leave her Raymond,' Lyn said firmly. 'She needs rest. She needs to go to hospital.'

'No, Mum. I must finish.'

'She is the only one, Mrs Thorne. I care for her, we all do. She'll be all right.'

'And how in God's name can you be so sure?'

'Exactly that, Mrs Thorne. In God's name.'

'I didn't think you were that religious, Raymond.'

'It makes no difference, if we truly believe, right now, she will be guided, she'll be all right.'

145

'I remember.' Melissa pulled away and sat bolt upright.

Enoch came closer, kneeling before her as if she were a queen. 'You remember the names?'

Melissa nodded. 'Fallen Angels, demonic powers, so pure but so evil. Lucifer – only heard the name. The others were Azazel – he was the leader. Morax was a teacher and looked kinda like a bull, but like a man. There was a woman – she was beautiful. She is called the Child of Lilith, pure evil. And Vapula – a powerful spirit.'

'Wow, that's some crazy stuff, sis.' Reuben worked his fingers fast on his phone. You know that's five demons, five again.'

'Five demons of Purgatory,' Enoch shifted his specs.

'These names, ah,.....found one. wow, sis.'

Lyn leant over him, studying the phone. 'What does it say?'

Reuben read fast. 'Azazel – sympathized with Satan, cast down to Earth, ruler of demons, also a character in Marvel comics. What was the other, Mor.. Mora..'

'Morax.' Melissa then repeated. 'Morax, Child of Lilith and Vapula.'

Reuben found them. 'Morax, man with head of bull, disguises himself in human form and teaches arts, science, and stuff. Lilith was, wow! Oh man, she was nasty, according to the books of Isaiah and Enoch.....' he stopped, directing his glance towards the man from Rome.

'Enoch?'

Reuben continued to read about the demons. 'Lilith was the first adulterer, related to Adam, steals babies. Wicked. Ah, she had a child – only known as The Child

146

of Lilith. Nothing about her. What was the the last name again?'

'Vapula.'

'It says here, warrior king, a teacher in human form, and a great Duke of the Underworld. Nice bunch.'

'They use weakened souls like Dexter to enter our world. They will use any portal, any time, and they will take human form, just as Satan does.' Enoch had heard of these demons. 'Evil fallen Angels, whom I would agree to call.....evil demons.'

Stan took a glass of water and offered it to Melissa. She took and sipped and studied the clear liquid.

'It's clear to me, like this water. I can see everything now. I'll go back in.'

Stan cleared his throat. 'You said that Dexter is in battle with these demons. Why did Dexter paint this picture, why did he let in the demons in the first place?'

'Mr Thorne, as mentioned, he was weak, unhappy and the painting, well I guess that was the way in. Don't forget, this is not of our realm.'

'Enoch,' Stan sighed. 'Realm? What are you talking about? Who uses words like *realm*?'

'Dad, leave it. Mr Raphael is our way through this, and I can help by allowing myself back to Dexter.'

Melissa, book in hand, current page, began to read. The air swirled, bright flashes bounced around the room.

'I'll turn the pages to see what we have to do.'

'No! Stop!' Stan yelled. 'Don't look.'

'He's right sis, you know why.' Reuben threw a look of doubt at Raymond. 'Should she look? And anyway, I thought the pages were blank. Could she *really* change the future?'

'Reuben, firstly the pages are blank to a non-believer. But if Melissa turns the page she may be able to read ahead, never know it might give us a little guidance. As for changing the future, well it's all about causality and determinism – they are changeable 'cos it's what we do all the time. But the book is already written – a *pre-determined* future. These events are already set. You can't change that. If you did somehow change something, when we get there, to that exact point in the future, we will cause a paradox of unimaginable power. You said it yourself - how can a future that is written, be already written if you change it.'

'Like when someone goes back in time and changes something and re-writes the future, the *past future*. Like in Back to the Future, the old film; he interferes with the past, stops his parents from meeting and nearly erases his own existence. Great movie.'

Raymond grinned. 'We've all seen it. It's the ripple effect. And yes, you're right – in this timeline there would be a paradox in the opposite direction – not past but future. Don't forget, time exists in all directions equally. It's only.....' Raymond stopped. 'Never mind, look, Melissa, just read. Free your mind and meet Dexter again. Ask for his guidance.'

Lyn glanced up at the ceiling. 'Here goes.'

'You seem remarkably calm, Enoch,' added Stan. 'Will it work?'

'It's all part of the bigger picture,' Enoch replied. 'Pieces of the puzzle. I am certain we can fit everything together. Timelines, paradoxes, visions, possessions, different dimensions – all of it. It'll fit neatly together. Trust me.'

Lyn was still unsure, 'Enoch, didn't you perform some sort of miracle earlier? Can't you do something, maybe talk to Dexter, or someone?'

'I wish it were that simple. Laws of another

dimension are strict. The Egyptians called it the Underworld, Christian belief says Purgatory, in Islam, Barzakh. This unknown place was something of myths and legend until now. I cannot go there. Melissa was chosen. She is pure, innocent. I am a priest, I would not be welcome in there.'

Reuben's phone light flashed as a message appeared. It was from a friend. The friend had asked how he was, having not seen him for a while. He then mentioned some breaking news.

'Text from my friend. People, the church is on fire, didn't those paramedics say something about that?'

Stan looked out the window and saw faint smoke. 'Yup. She must have been given another.... I dunno, you answer that Enoch.'

Enoch nodded. 'I did have guidance, yet I do not know from whom. I gave the visions to her.'

'Well I hope everyone is all right.' Stan glanced towards the hallway with the open front door. 'That painting starts to burn, then the church. What next? We have got to stop this, stop the demons. Let's do it.'

So, Melissa refocused on the words in the book, briefly re-reading prior events and then in real-time. It was now. Everything she read, was happening right now.

The Painting had stopped smouldering. There was a gaping hole where the church once stood. The gravestones were all blank, unwritten names of those who would soon die.

# Chapter Twenty One

## Speaking in Tongues

'Dexter, I am with you again. It's me, Melissa. I can feel the cool water, the gentle breeze. There are birds. It is beautiful. I can feel the gentle grip of your hand. I can hear you. Tell me how we must finish this.'

In Dexter's own voice, Melissa spoke.

'Use your sixth sense to open your subconscious mind, allow the good Angels in. Then you must all speak in tongues of forgotten script, secondary languages of the Angels. You will know these languages as you are true believers. I have met a great man, one who yields wondrous power. He will guide your voices. Together we will cast out the demons from this beautiful place and send them back to Sheol. Let's begin.'

Melissa broke off and looked at everyone.

'Sixth sense? You don't *really* believe in the sixth sense do you?' Lyn asked Enoch.

'Ever sensed someone was watching you, then turned round and someone is? Ever thought about somebody and seconds later a message appears, from them? Have you seen Jasper bark at a blank wall? Goosebumps for no apparent reason? And it's quite common for a loved one to sense someone is ill, had an accident or even died, yet they are many miles away. There's also that old saying *my ears are burning*; your sixth sense indicates that someone is talking about you.'

'Okay, but what has this got to do with everything.'

'Jigsaw, Lyn. You'll see. Now open your mind.'

Each member of the family, together with Enoch and Raymond, simultaneously began to speak in tongues of Aramaic, ancient Latin and Akkadian.

"Non cogit ut Deum perpot entiam."

"Dumaya D'Shiado aarpea b'hadea b'ealma."

Shaytan ghadar lana, Allah 'Akbar."

"....exorcizo te immundissime spíritus."

"In nomine Domini nostrosi Jesus Christi."

"....te Alaha d ahrima d diqata."

"Shaytan ghadar hdha almakan."

"The power of us all compels you."

"Dexter Manning, alsalam'ealaykum."

"Dexter Manning, peace be upon you."

Another surreal moment ended with complete silence. Melissa closed the book and smiled for the first time for hours, or what felt like days. It was a beautiful moment. Perfect calm, not the calm before the storm, but peace.

Enoch had yet another revelation, yet one he had already known. All religions, every one, came from the same source, and in any moment of suffering, all nations fight as one. Yet, he also had a moment of doubt. Although he did not doubt the rite of exorcism, he was unsure that they would see the last of the demons.

Time was running out.

Jasper had remained calm throughout this, again upstairs, waiting for his own moment. He rushed down, heavy footed on the stairway carpet, barking loudly.

Stan pulled at the others who followed hastily to the front door. Jasper stood over a wooden frame lying on the gravel by the wall. It was the frame from the painting, with no canvas, nothing. The Painting had gone.

'Wait,' Melissa disappeared momentarily and returned with the book. She glanced around for approval. She turned straight to page 152. She needed to see what was next, what was to come.

As expected, there were written words of what was happening in the present. She allowed her eyes to roll to the very bottom of the page. It said,

*patientia est virtus*

'That was all very interesting.'

The voice came from the end of the footpath, startling them all. Standing tall was Inspector Farley with Paula Shelby from the station. 'We seem to be spending a lot of time around this street. Care to explain why neighbours have called us regarding a 'noisy disturbance?''

'Sorry officers,' Stan moved up to greet them, shaking Farley's hand.

'We were also asked to take a look, following a mysterious call to paramedics.'

'Yeah, it's all sorted now. Everyone is fine. I mean, Melissa, my daughter is fine.'

'May we come in?' asked Paula Shelby.

There was nothing abnormal; an old picture frame outside, an odd burn mark on the wall. Nothing else. It almost looked like a show-house it was so tidy. A simple wall clock read 10:57. 'There is one thing; we heard chanting in foreign languages. Care to explain?'

'We were rehearsing for a university, um play.'

Raymond looked dumbfounded. He quickly came in, 'Oh that's right, I study Para....religion, got this play at the theatre. Just rehearsing.'

'Did I hear Latin?' Farley asked.

'Yes, well old Latin.'

'You must be pretty brainy to remember Latin, what was it you said you were studying?'

'Science. And religion. And not just Latin anyway, other old languages too.'

'Wow, I'm impressed.'

Paula spotted Jasper coming up to her. 'Lovely dog.'

'Jasper,' Stan said. 'Very intelligent, great company.'

'We have a colleague, we call him Billy, who adores

dogs. Loves them to bits.'

Stan offered up the seats and both detectives sat down graciously. 'I know Billy, well I don't know him, just read about him – you call him Billy the Kid.'

Paula threw a look of surprise, 'How is that possible?' She frowned.

Farley checked the names on his mobile database: they were all squeaky clean – even his *own* record wasn't as clean as theirs.

Lyn was about to offer a coffee to the guests when she noticed something odd. 'Mr Raphael, you all right?'

Enoch looked unstable on his feet. He clutched his head, pressed his thumbs into his temples and cried out in agony. The searing pain attacked his inner-most thoughts, his brain felt heavy.

Lyn beckoned Stan to help her walk Enoch to a seat, but the priest refused.

'I'm fine. Just a headache.'

Lyn moved into the kitchen to make coffee. Some seconds later, a loud bang and a crack of thunder had the two officers leap up from their seats. Lyn poured boiling water over the worktop, just missing her hand. She knocked over the coffee pot and ran back into the living room.

Enoch looked different somehow. He seemed to focus on infinity, looking right through them. He spoke, softly and calmly, Biblically. 'Do not fear my friends for I have always known my destiny, this day has come, all that I have learnt and all that I am, is power, power of good to wage war on the evil that tears through this world.' He stood tall, stretching, arms outreached. 'I told you that there shall be a trade – a soul for a soul. And our Lord formed my body from the dust and into it breathed divine breath. For one purpose alone. I am as

154

bright as the light of lightning through the sky, and with me shall come our King, who shall fall as a great star on this day. This day has come.'

'What the hell?' Farley wore an expression of intrigue. 'What was all that?'

'Raymond, my son, come to me.'

'Mr Raphael?' Raymond moved closer. He felt Enoch's hand touch his shoulder and a thousand visions raced through his mind. He did not pull away despite the pain. Raymond spoke in an oddly old-timey way. 'Enoch, you were awaiting an opening into the next world. I know, it is Earth, all of us. The underworld, Hades, Purgatory, and Heaven. They are all places on Earth – all around us. Different times, different dimensions. I didn't know before as I was blind to the truth but now I see you Father. You are the one. You must go, for I shall carry on your work to the far reaches of Earth. You go, rid this place of evil, remove the demonic Angels and banish them, destroy them, cease this infernal rampage set upon the Earth. Rid us all of our sins.'

Enoch spoke for the last time;

**'Ego hic apud vos Jesus Christus resistere diabolo. Amen.'**

Another clap of thunder rang through the house, a flash as bright as lightning took away their vision. Then there was complete silence. Rubbing their sore eyes, the Thorne family, and the detectives spotted one figure laying dormant on the living room floor.

'Raymond!' Melissa threw herself over the lifeless body. 'Ray, please wake up, Raymond,' she slapped him and began hitting him in a flood of tears.

Reuben pulled her away, 'Let me see him, move!'

Stan crouched down. 'He's moving.' He felt a pulse, he felt breath. 'Raymond,' Stan said softly.

'I'm alive, but I've never felt worse.'

Relief swept across Melissa's face as she gripped his hand.'

'Um, guys,' Lyn said, staring at the floor. **'Where's Enoch?'**

Detective Farley beckoned his colleague Paula to move closer to where Enoch was standing. They both crouched down. Farley reached for a silver chain and cross. He picked it up and stood. With his palm out, Farley showed the others. 'If I wasn't a believer before, I sure am now.'

'What d'you think it means Sir?' Paula enquired.

'I'll fill you in on that,' Raymond eased his weary body up with Melissa and Stan's assistance.

'I was never really a believer, a religious man. I don't recall ever talking like that, like just now. But, I saw something, not just a flash of light, but I saw into his mind. That's why I said that I must carry on his work. I don't mean paranormal activity, I mean *his* work.'

'But did you see.....' Lyn tried hard to believe it all, but she new that her eyes had not deceived her, nor did she imagine what she had heard, '....did you see where he went?'

'No. But this,' Raymond pointed at the Cross of Christ in the palm of the detective's hand. 'This – this is a sign. It's all he left us, in this world. It's for me.' Raymond took the chain and carefully put it around his neck, cross down, Christ facing out from his chest.

Reuben sat down in the comfortable leather armchair, it may have been a wooden bench, he had little physical feeling now. 'Tell me, *who is* Enoch?'

Raymond grinned. 'He is a messenger of God, he is the one.'

'The chosen one?' Lyn asked innocently. 'Is he Christ?'

Raymond laughed. 'Goodness no! Don't you recall his words just now?'

Lyn gave a dumbfounded expression and shrugged her shoulders.

'Ray,' Melissa gripped his hand tighter. 'This is all very, um, difficult for us to understand. This is a new experience for us. I don't think any of us knew what you were both saying. It was really weird, and then the thunder and....'

'Let me stop you there.' Raymond took a deep breath and exhaled slowly. 'This is all new to me too. Remember when we spoke in strange old languages? All the weird events that have happened? It's all pretty much scary for me too ya know. You're not alone.'

'You haven't answered my question,' Reuben added.

'I'm sorry. To answer that I would need you all to understand something. Remember the old stories we were taught about Satan and his so called fallen Angels?'

There were half-hearted nods of agreement.

'Fallen Angels, demons, bad spirits expelled from Heaven have been walking among us, living within this world for all of mankind's history. The demons, or bad angels we witnessed over the last few days, prey upon the weak and lonely, preaching their works through the arts, through astrology, science and astronomy. They can enter the body of the weak and take control of a soul the moment the body dies. This is how Morax, I believe, took control of Dexter.'

'But didn't we agree Dexter was fighting the

demons?' Melissa asked.

'Yeah; sometimes there's still enough energy from the dead – this can come forward, if you like, and fight the Demon.'

'As with Dexter,' Stan added.

Raymond nodded. 'And he left us clues didn't he? The names on the gravestones, the five-star pentagram with the Latin script on the wall?'

Lyn shook her head. 'Not buying this, sorry. They weren't clues they were horrible scare tactics.'

'Remember it is very hard for a, how can I put this, a dead person to communicate.'

Lyn exchanged looks with her husband. They were looks of bewilderment, confusion and exhaustion.

'Come on everyone I think we need to take some time out.' Stan motioned the detectives to sit down. 'Your report is going to be mighty interesting detectives.'

Farley stared at the floor as he sat in the sofa alongside Paula. 'There'll be no report.'

Nobody said a thing. It was plain and simple. The detectives could not file a report of such unbelievable calibre.

'What would I write? *We arrived at a disturbance following an unusual emergency response for paramedics. Upon arrival we witnessed ancient Latin spoken, Godly visions and the arrival and departure of a chosen angel sent to fight a demon, with claps of thunder and a bolt of lightning said man disappears.*

Not sure if anyone would believe that down at the station.'

Paula smiled. 'Tim, I think that we should report that paramedics had been in attendance following the collapse of a sixteen year old girl. Three other family members and the young girl's friend were also at the

158

scene. There were no domestic disturbances.'

Farley took her hand and suddenly let go, having again realised how unprofessional it was. 'Absolutely. There were five of you here,' he looked straight at the others. 'Melissa collapsed from an unknown cause, and she has agreed to be seen by her doctor tomorrow,' he nodded for her to agree. 'They were in the process of learning ancient Latin for a theatrical play and noise heard from neighbours can be justified by simply saying you got carried away and that you are indeed very sorry. Okay?'

'What about the thunder and lightning or whatever that was?' Reuben added.

'Sound effects. Look, how well do you know your neighbours? I'm sure they'll accept that you're rehearsing for a play at university.'

Raymond agreed. The others nodded in unison. It was settled. Nothing of the recent events would ever be spoken about again.

'And what about Enoch?' Raymond asked.

'He was never here.'

'I think he would want this. He's gone to a different place, somewhere we can't imagine, to begin his journey, so yeah, he was never here.'

'I'm going to ask one more time,' Reuben muttered. 'WHO is he?'

Raymond looked over to Reuben, rolled his eyes around the room and back. He clutched the silver cross. 'HE is Archangel Enoch Raphael, a great man, a prophet, and an angel of peace.'

# Chapter Twenty Two

## Possessed

'Oh my God! Guys, you have got to see this.'

Stan came outside to meet his wife. 'How did that happen? The painting is back.'

'Did we all just imagine the painting had burnt?'

'If that's true, God alone knows what else we've all imagined.'

'That's more than worrying, isn't it?' Lyn added.

Reuben appeared. 'How do we know *anything* is real?'

'Exactly,' replied Stan.

'Yeah but Enoch is not here, I mean he's still, not *here*,' Lyn replied. 'It's real. Take a look at the churchyard – look at the gravestones.'

'All blank but one. Enoch - his name is there.'

'So he *is* dead?'

'Hey, look over there,' Stan pointed. 'Smoke from the church fire. That was real. Those paramedics said there was a fire.'

Raymond thought deeply, then said 'If that's real, it means that we *are in* reality, but then how did the painting turn back to its original self?'

'How can we tell if this is reality or a collective vision?'

'Stan, I am still wearing the cross that Enoch dropped.'

'That means nothing – we all know just how real our visions have been – this could be reality or another dream.'

'You mean Nightmare,' Lyn added.

'If the painting is back, yet the church is really on fire, and we are indeed in a reality....'

'You thinking what I'm thinking?' Reuben asked.

'We are all thinking it, Reuben.'

'The Demon is back.'

'And Enoch died for nothing.'

'Maybe not. Many say that about Jesus but it doesn't stop people believing.'

'Is he still out there somewhere, in a different time?'

A sudden flash blinded them temporarily and Melissa fell to her knees. She screamed out for Dexter.

'What now?' Stan yelled. 'Melissa?'

Melissa dropped her head and then turned to face her father. Her head seemed to keep turning. Her neck muscles cracked.

'Christ!' Stan grabbed her head but with a truly powerful force, Melissa threw him back against the living room wall, his head collected the corner of the tall display cabinet, sending glass animal ornaments and a family portrait crashing to the floor. Stan fell like jelly. The beige carpet began to soak up a new red.

Lyn reached for her daughter and was greeted by a deep, haunting, demonic growl. Lyn froze, not by her own doing, but involuntarily, an arm stretched out towards Melissa. She could not move any part of her body, she could form no sounds. She remained statuesque, her limbs began turning to brittle stone. Her brain registered everything, the pain, the emotion, the hell.

'Look what you made me do,' Melissa's demonic form growled. 'Enoch made me burn, but he did not win and now you will pay.'

Reuben moved a step closer to Melissa. 'Leave her and go back to hell.'

'Oh my dear child, hell is just a word. Reality is so

161

much worse.'

Reuben felt a burning pain radiating through every nerve in his body until he collapsed, his nervous system had failed. He was looking directly at his demonic sister and could feel nothing from his body. He felt absolutely nothing but mental agony, that began to fade.

Using Melissa's form, the demon Morax spoke in a gravelly tone again. 'You will die for your sins, you interfered with my teachings for the last time Enoch Raphael. Watch your puny little friends die, horribly.'

Raymond and the two detectives were the only remaining fully-conscious and mobile ones left. 'Detectives, what should we do?'

'Aren't you some kind of expert?' Paula asked.

'Not when it comes to this, no.'

'Oh, come now. My love, Raymond. I know you want me, you always have. Come closer. You want this girl don't you? Feast of desire upon her delicate nubile flesh?'

'Get away from her, let her go.'

'Oh I'm afraid there's nothing left of her now, but you only wanted her beauty, her perfect body, I mean, what else did she have?'

'That's not true, it's not true!'

'Look inside you Raymond, do you not want eternal life with her? I can give that, if you desire.'

'You disgust me.'

Morax laughed using Melissa's own body, and with her voice, seductively asked, 'Ray, honey, spend eternity with me, there will be no time – for time will cease to exist. There will be no suffering, no death. Just pleasure. Join us, we have such wonderful sights to show you.'

Raymond yelled to the detectives. 'This is not real. SAY IT!'

They all chanted together, repeating and repeating. 'This is not real, we are not here, this is not real, this is just our minds.....'

'Ha! You think this is not real?' Morax laughed. 'Oh this is real. So very real. Didn't you see the smoke? That was real. And you see that dead body over there – could have been your future father-in-law. Oh he's real. And now that we've accepted fate, and our futures, let's move on, shall we?'

'I want my friends back.'

'Forget them, they are your past. We are your future.'

*　　*

Hamden police station had been busy. Two units had been called to the church fire to carry out investigations into possible arson. The local fire crews contained the fire and the church received only superficial damage, yet the chancel and part of the nave had been damaged. The church warden and Reverend Harris had been treated for mild smoke inhalation and were with the two paramedics when a new young constable began asking questions. Unusually, Sergeant Bonné had been sent along too. Despite being firearm certified, he was also a regular Bobbie and still required to do, what he referred to as, boring work.

The Reverend had not seen any suspicious activity, nor heard any unusual sounds. The fire simply 'roared up like a lion, right there, in front of me,' he announced, trembling. 'It was fire from hell.'

Bonné held back a grin. 'Okay, thank you Reverend, you get yourself checked out down at the hospital.'

The two policemen walked away, but turned back upon hearing the Reverend shout. 'They are here. The

163

five demons are here! Here on earth!'

Bonné nodded to Reverend Harris and pulled his young officer away. 'Screw loose or what?'

Immediately following this, an even more unusual interruption came bouncing toward them. A Golden Retriever dog.

'Well, howdy partner, whatcha doing in this neck o'the woods?' William called out, 'Anyone know who's dog this is?'

'I do.'

They turned back to face the reverend, he spoke softly, 'His name is Jasper and he belongs to the Thorne family, number five Pines Avenue.'

William nodded. 'Okay thanks Vicar.'

'Sir,' another officer called. 'Sergeant Bonné.'

'Stop calling everyone sir. And call me William, or Bill. Not Sir.'

'Okay, but the station has lost contact with Inspector Shelby and Inspector Farley. They're not answering any calls. And there have been several reports from neighbours about screams and loud bangs.'

'Hey slow down there speedy, you're talking as fast as a train. Have you tried to contact them?'

'Just this minute. Nothing, nada.'

'You say neighbours? Where are they at?'

'They went to meet paramedics who were called to an unusual response – five Pines Avenue.'

William exchanged a surprised look with his new constable. 'Five. Well ain't that a dandy. Best go check it out.' William called to the other officers; 'I'm on this, you guys stay here. I'm sure it's nothing.'

As William began to enter the patrol car, he sensed something brushing against him. Jasper barked and clambered inside. 'Come on right in there why don't you? Y'a get me shot by the sheriff don't y'a know. But hey, come along for the ride, take ya back to yo mama now.' He glanced at the car's clock; 11:05.

Upon arrival a few minutes later, William and Jasper came across several worried-looking neighbours. He said nothing and as they stared at the policeman, Jasper bolted for the open door.

William heard an awful, gut-wrenching yelp, a whimper followed by a terrified scream, a female scream. The female voice cried out, 'Oh God no, why did you do that?'

The response was haunting, a shiver ran down William's spine. His neck hairs stood on end. He knew the female voice. It was her. He admired, truly admired Paula. 'Move back!' he screamed at the neighbours. 'Everyone get inside your homes and lock the doors, shut the windows. GO!'

'I will kill all of you, one by one, but you will suffer at my pleasure,' said the demonic voice.

With the onlookers scattering, William called in. 'This is sergeant Bonné 141881 calling for immediate backup, five Pines avenue. I say again five Pines, Papa India November Echo Sierra. Possible violent disturbance and threats heard. All units respond. AFO legal, requesting authorisation for use of firearm, over.'

William crept inside, slowly, stealthily. His heartbeat pounding. He saw the back end of Jasper motionless on the hallway carpet. He reversed himself out and edged along to the front window.

He gasped and threw himself back against the wall. To hell with protocol, he thought. He wasn't going to wait for the Central Firearms Team to relay a message to Hamden station, and what if they did not give him authority? He scampered back to the car, unlocked a special floor panel in the trunk of the Toyota and withdrew a Glock 17 pistol.

William crept back to the house. His mind was racing. Okay, he'd taken specialist training to be the authorised firearms officer for the entire area, but never had he thought he'd need it. He had also never seen such a scene as he had just witnessed through the window. There appeared to be at least one dead. A young woman kneeling down facing away from the window. And a dead dog.

'Oh Christ this is it, this stuff is real,' he said to himself.

'Come on right inside and join the party, why don't ya, Billy.'

The voice was throaty and gravelly, yet with an oddly female tone.

'How do you know who I am?' he replied, still not fully inside the hallway.

'I am the all-seeing eye, and I have already seen this. I know all about you Billy. Think you're a big shot wild-west cowboy do ya?'

William was ultra nervous, sweat formed upon his brow. He gripped the gun firmly, swung round the hallway wall and into the living room.

'God-damn you I will fire!'

'And whom shall you shoot, Billy?'

That was a good question. The demonic voice seemed to come from the girl, still kneeling, facing slightly away. He glanced over at Farley and Paula Shelby then nodded. He collected his thoughts together, quickly. The scene; a male, possibly forties, severe head trauma, dead. Teenage boy, lying on side, lifeless, no sign of movement, dead. A woman, possibly forty, in an unusual stance, partial kneeling, leaning forward, arm stretched. Like a statue. And another male, around

166

twenty, pressed up against the wall, panting in fear. Shattered glass on the blood-stained floor. What appeared to be burn marks on the carpet, a blown light bulb, and a single book lying on the carpet, titled, The Painting, the moody cover picture was Hamden church, where he had been just ten minutes ago.

'Tim, Sir,' William's voice quivered. 'Sir, what shall I do?'

'Hey you wanna see something cool?' asked Morax. The demon snapped off Lyn's arm like a twig and still with Melissa's hand, pulled the still conscious Lyn closer. With another snap, the demon broke her neck and she tumbled down.

'Jesus!' William cried.

Farley managed to say some heart-breaking words. 'Shoot her, it's the only way. The girl is dead, what you see is not the girl but a demon. It's what caused the fire at the church. It's done all this. We are all going to die anyway. Shoot it, Billy, shoot it.'

No way on this earth would William shoot an unarmed young woman. But his mind visualised the previous moments at the church. The Reverend said something about a demon. The dog suddenly appears. Paula and Tim are missing. Neighbours had called in about a disturbance. And now, there were dead people, and a dead dog, and some strange weird, evil stuff going on.

'Go on, Billy, I know you want to,' Morax said. 'Ever killed before?'

William couldn't believe his eyes as the young woman's head turned more than ninety degrees, hollow black eyes in pale grey skin. Frothy blood oozing from mouth and nostrils. He froze.

Paula remembered her vision. Dexter had touched her – and she had been given the visions. She had seen

167

a young woman with hollow black eyes, but she had also seen her death. And she knew that she would now die at the hand of Billy. 'Dexter Manning,' she said solemnly. 'Help us. I know who you are – our connection is deep – granny Dot was your sister. Dexter, you must help, we are family.' She turned to Billy. 'Please,' she cried, 'Please don't kill me.'

'Oh, live it up, cowboy, Billy the Kid. You can join me forever, live in bliss, tasting the pure delight of whatever flesh you desire, time standing still, no seconds, no hours, no days, pure eternal bliss. Shoot. Empty that gun. You know she's dead, what harm could it do?'

Sirens could be heard.

'Oh detectives, Mr Kid, your friends are here. More flesh for me to enjoy.'

'What the hell are you?' William asked calmly.

'I AM hell.'

'You're evil.'

'No, that is pretence of humanity, your immediate response to something different.' The demon looked at Raymond. 'If you like I could teach you the real meaning of life, no false teachings about Christ, don't you want to know why we exist? The universe, where it all began? I was there at the beginning of time, before your God. I was one of the few. But I was cast out like an old worn robe. Lucifer took me under his wing. But for millennia after millennia I have suffered under the weight of the Christ. Then he came to Earth, the chosen one indeed. He was not the begotten son. He is nothing.'

'Shut up!' Raymond screamed. 'You lie!'

'Raymond, I know you understand. You have always sought truth, and meaning. You have always believed in the paranormal, the cause and causality. Determinism, my boy. Everything you have ever done, has a meaning, an effect, it determines your next step. And this one, is now. This is your destiny, Raymond. You are mine.'

'Shut the hell up or I *will* shoot you.'

'Oh, Billy, Billy. Poor old Billy. In love with a woman nearly twice your age. She's right here don't you know. Go on, it's causality, express your true feeling, you must.'

William glanced over at Paula who was whimpering, her head buried in Tim's arms.

'If you do not seize this moment Billy, then the next logical step in time's causality is for you to renounce your desires for her. So you must kill her.'

'What?'

William felt pressure on him, his arms felt heavy, his body began to turn. He could not control his movements however hard he tried. He fought for control, failing, failing. His arm raised. His right index finger began to squeeze the trigger, just gently, slowly. The Glock pistol aimed at Paula's body.

'No, please, stop, stop....' Paula wept.

William cried out, desperately fighting the demon.

Paula jolted away from Tim, towards the window. The trigger squeezed. Bang.

Paula's head bounced sideways spraying blood in a neat line over the glass. She fell to the floor. Tim collapsed over her. William regained control and screamed abuse, hurling every bad word he could think of. He was unaware of the arrival of four officers.

'NO!' one officer screamed.

William did not hear.

'William, don't do it.'

It was too late.

William fired three shots into the head, neck and torso of Melissa. He then quickly tuned the gun,

169

pressed it into the roof of his mouth and squeezed the trigger again. His body jolted backwards violently spraying blood and skull fragment over the living room wall and the clock, that read 11:15

# Chapter Twenty Three

# Time Running Out

At the police station, Farley was being questioned. It felt strange being the *other* side of the table. He'd questioned dozens of people, he knew what to expect. Gently polite questions, then a bit firmer, more direct. Then there would be a few sales tactics, *'it would be in your best interest to tell us everything, withholding truth will land you in more hot water, blah blah blah.'*

The inspector did tell the SO everything, whether he believed it or not wasn't important. Farley knew what he had seen. It was an appalling turn of events, strange, almost unexplainable actions, the demons at work. There wasn't anything he could not believe. He saw it all with his own eyes. Latin rites of exorcism, flashes of light, rumbles of thunder, possession of a young woman, violent murders. And his colleagues; he knew that Billy would not have shot Paula in any sane state of mind. He looked demonic as he pointed the gun, it almost appeared as if he were battling against his arm, struggling to prevent his finger squeezing on the trigger. Farley pictured the living room – what a mess. Blood and skin over the wall. Paula's blood over the window. Two female victims on the floor, one with limbs missing, the other with a soul missing. The father, neck broken, lying in his own blood upon the carpet. A teenage boy, lifeless. And the pet dog, neck broken, on the floor between living room and hallway. Then the burn marks over the wall and on the floor from those bolts of lightning. Everything was there for forensics, no more evidence needed. Neighbours had called in reports of noise, loud bangs, flashes, screams. So he knew that there would be nothing imagined or made up. Unfortunately, there were no other witnesses to the original mayhem. Raymond would be held for a long time. As for Farley, he knew that forensics would easily place the shooting squarely on Billy.

What else could he add? They could let him go for now.

The door to the holding room creaked and opened. Farley hated the word cell; the *holding room* was far more welcoming. A Chief Inspector from central had taken over, it was always best to have independent officers run an internal investigation. Safer that way, much fairer. The officer announced that he would be free to leave once a few more paperwork checks were done.

'What about the young man, Raymond Shaw?'

'His story is identical to yours, checks out. Still, he's going to be here for a while.'

'Why are you holding him?'

'Only witness. There from the start, saw everything.'

'I know.'

Farley understood, yet he wondered about Enoch. Had Raymond mentioned anything about him? He hoped not; another man, a 'vanishing' man would lead to even more questions. They might never get out. And he needed to get out, with Raymond and solve this right now, before his mind faltered, before the shock of seeing two close colleagues shot to death. Now was the time.

The Chief asked Farley to follow him out. Before he reached the door, Tim stopped.

'I need to get back on this investigation. Can I have another word with Raymond?'

'Against protocol, Sir.'

'Of course it is,' Farley muttered sarcastically under his breath.

The minutes passed by and Tim Farley was beginning to feel the shock wearing off. The sights he witnessed were playing havoc on his mind. He began to become emotional, but held back. He had already refused counselling and signed a waiver for it. Counselling would waste valuable time. But he needed an excuse to stick around, to get an opportunity to see young Raymond.

'Excuse me, I'm not leading the investigation but I am the best person who can help. Actually, Raymond Shaw is not just the key witness, but probably the only one with expertise in what went down.'

'Not sure what you mean Inspector Farley. He kept mentioning demons. He's crazy, d'you expect me to take this lad seriously? We're talking about a multiple murder investigation here.'

'I mentioned demonic possession, too. Am I crazy? You going to force me to see counselling?'

The Chief shook his head.

'All right,' Farley added. 'Forensics – have them check out some burn marks on the wall. They did not come from any normal source.'

A sigh was followed by, 'Okay, okay. I'll call them.' He paused. 'Five minutes, all right. You can have five minutes with Mr Shaw.'

'Thanks, I'll get it done.'


Raymond was relieved to see Farley. He'd known him for only an hour and yet he felt like a friend.

'Inspector, glad to see you.'

'I have only five minutes.'

'Five?'

'Yes, five.'

'There's that magic number five again.'

Farley looked confused. 'Hey, whatever, look, I need to get you out before the Chief gets back.

'How are you going to do that? It's not exactly easy to break out of a police station.'

'Raymond, I outrank everyone here, and the Chief from HQ is busy right now.'

Farley peered out into the open-plan office.

'Well. Is it clear?'

'Not exactly. Look, the best way to commit a crime is in broad daylight in front of everyone. People never suspect a thing because nobody is dumb enough to do it. The perfect crime. So all we do is walk right out, calmly and leave.'

'Is that a thing? Is that for real? It won't work.'

Farley forced a smile. 'No, yes, and maybe. It's just what you hear in the movies. Just trying to keep you calm, that's all.'

'You're not helping, but there is something in your theory. Just pretend you're escorting me somewhere. As long as that Chief doesn't see us....'

'Now you're talking. Do exactly what I say.'

Farley led Raymond out of the holding room, across the office, casually collected a set of patrol vehicle keys and his light jacket, then informed the desk sergeant that he was escorting Mr Shaw to Room B.

'That was easy. Now, stop. Wait, wait. Okay, she's not looking, quick, through the door.'

They were outside with no suspicion. Job done. Farley and Raymond took no time finding the marked patrol car, a brand new Ford. It felt great, Farley, the DI for the station, committing a crime. Well, sort of a crime, he thought. All he had done was to release a man being held for questioning without authority. Although, he surmised, this was a multiple murder enquiry.

'Let's get the hell out of here, ditch the car and go from there.'

'Sounds good to me, Inspector.'

'Tim. Call me Tim, I'm no longer working for the police. Oh, and Raymond – think mighty hard about our plan of action.'

'I already have. We need to retrieve the painting. Last time I saw it, it was whole again – just outside the front door. I think that was a sign – a sign that says we can rebuild. The painting was gone, then it returned. I just wonder if, you know.'

'Right. Okay. What we'll do is....damn.'

'What?'

'I was going to just request it as evidence but forensics will need it, and to top that, by now word is out that we have escaped.'

'Escaped?'

'Well, basically, yeah.'

'Jesus. Whoops, I must stop saying that.' Raymond didn't want to tempt fate, or the devil, or whatever, by using Christ's name as a swear. 'I've got it! Hey, This may sound daft, but Jesus...Jesus can help. I'm not really religious, maybe a bit, but if we can get that painting to the grave of Dexter Manning, the energy created would enable us to, um, well, pray.'

'Still gotta get that painting.'

'Leave that to me.'

Tim parked up in a gateway to a field. 'Come on let's go by foot, we can cut across the wheat field. Raymond, I still don't really know enough about this case. I mean, okay, I saw that crazy stuff go down, the possession, but what the heck is so important about a painting?'

'Dexter Manning, the old man who died?'

175

'Yeah, I know that. He wrote me a letter after he died. Paula and I handled the case.'

'Well, he painted it. In it he painted his own grave. But somehow, through his own negative energy, he opened a portal to hell, or purgatory. He allowed demons in – they are all indirectly controlled by the devil.'

They both eased up and paused for breath.

'Go on, I'm with you so far.'

'Well, you know the Thorne family..........'

Raymond stopped. The reality of it suddenly hit him like a bus. They were dead – they were such a lovely family. Melissa....

Raymond couldn't hold back the tears. He barely managed to speak. 'Melissa was a great friend of mine.'

Tim put his hand on Raymond's shoulder. 'Sorry for your loss. You remember the other officer, Paula?' Raymond nodded. 'She and I were great friends too. I was about to ask her on a date. I hadn't because I thought I'd make a fool of myself, you know, at my age and all.'

'Tim, I learnt a lot from the priest, Enoch. He taught me so much. And I believe there is a way. Whatever we do, we MUST get that painting, go to the grave, summon Dexter and Enoch, and between us, now this is just theoretical, there's a way we can see them again.'

They continued, unsighted. Pines Avenue was awash with police, forensics and nosey neighbours. 'We can pretend, no, *you* can pretend you're just a nosey neighbour. Walk right up to the door and snatch the painting. Hang on, where is it?'

'Have they already taken it?'

'Okay, I know what to do.'

The men wandered up to some onlookers. 'Excuse

me,' Tim said. 'Have you seen a painting being carried away?'

Shakes of heads were all they achieved from the neighbours.

'Kids. Look over there. Kids see everything and you know something, they tell the truth more often than adults. Now there's a fact. We'll ask them.'

Raymond went up to three kids on bikes, 'How long have you been here? Seen anything?'

'We've been here ages, heard the screams from my house.'

'Yeah, heard gunshots too.'

The young boys and the girl were genuine. They had seen everything, and no painting had been carried away.

'Hey, how about doing some investigation for us?' Raymond asked.

'Have you been crying?' asked the girl.

Raymond couldn't deny it. 'I was upset when I heard. I was a friend of theirs.'

'You know what happened?'

Raymond faced the kids. 'Go to the door and ask, find out for me.'

'No way, I ain't going down there, I'll get in trouble with the cops.'

Farley came over. His jacket covered his hi-vis and any real evidence of him being a policeman. 'Twenty pounds in it for you?'

For twenty pounds, the two boys snuck over to the house and straight up to the crime scene, where they were greeted by police, and asked to leave immediately. It was enough time to scan the place.

Upon returning one boy stated, 'There's a picture of a church or something, in the hallway.'

The young girl piped up, 'Did you see any dead bodies?'

'No. I don't wanna anyway.'

Tim thanked the kids and led Raymond away. 'Right, Raymond. How are you with disguises?'

'Did a fancy dress party last year. Went as Captain America.'

'O...kay, look; everyone's out here, watching. It's a sunny day. Clothes on lines?'

'Let's check.'

There wasn't much success; and sneaking into back gardens was going to arouse suspicion – in an area of a crime scene. That plan was torn up.

'For heaven's sake, Tim. Do any of those cops and forensics look familiar? Would they know me?'

'Can't see anyone I know well, recognise one or two. Nobody would recognise you, still, those kids got turned away fast. If it was my crime scene I'd go nuts if anyone got within fifty metres. Seriously.'

'Yes or no? Shall I go?'

'Yes.' Farley rubbed his chin. 'I'll distract them.'

'How?'

'Don't you worry about that, just walk right up to..'

'No, Inspector, Tim. I know a way in through the back. Let me have your white shirt and hi-vis.'

Being roughly the same size, the swap was perfect. Tucked behind trees and near to a set of garages, they swapped clothes. Donned in a police hi-vis vest and black uniform trousers, Raymond dodged around two parked cars, along a short ally and up to number five. Nobody there, up and over the fence. In. Now to the back door. He brushed past two forensic officers in the kitchen who were making coffee. Raymond looked twice, were they really making coffee? A good sign, he guessed – they were busy. He stopped, dared himself to look the part. 'One for me while you're at it, going to be here for a while. Milk, two sugars.'

'No probs, we'll leave it on the table.'

'Unbelievable,' Raymond muttered to himself.

Two uniformed officers stood next to the painting. 'Damn, too close. Come on Farley, where's the distraction?'

And there it was, right on cue.

A house alarm across the street, number eight was wailing, high-pitched noise.

The two police officers at the front porch wandered up the path to see what was happening. Raymond grabbed the painting that was in a neat clear plastic bag, and walked, calmly out through the kitchen. He grabbed the coffee, said thanks to the forensic guys and went out through the back door. The two forensic officers gave quizzed looks, yet said nothing.

'Well done my boy,' Tim Farley said, patting Raymond on the back. 'Now, leg it, you've tampered with a crime scene and I've just set off someone's house alarm.'

# Chapter Twenty Four

## Tempus-Iterum

The two had escaped, ran for several minutes, and collapsed in exhaustion. Mental and physical exhaustion.

'The church – it's not far,' Tim said. 'Come on. We can deal with consequences later – they'll soon start panicking 'cos they've lost valuable evidence, oh and the Chief will be going ape by now. But first we have demons of our own.'

They arrived at the church and found Dexter's grave. It was freshly laid. On the simple headstone were his name and dates. Then the words, 'In God's keeping.'

'Was he a religious man?' asked Tim.

'No idea, never knew him.'

'Okay, now what,?' Tim propped the painting up against the grave. The portrait was indeed highly accurate. 'He's even painted his own gravestone exactly. How did he know? And look at the details on the church, everything right down to the......ah!'

Both felt electricity flow through them. 'What the hell?'

Nobody else was nearby, no sound, not even a bird. It seemed to turn darker yet there were few clouds. Both men looked up, naturally, almost expecting a solar eclipse. Then, a cool breeze rustled up a few leaves.

A voice spoke inside their minds, both simultaneously.

'You have come, my friends, as I had foreseen.

Thank you my son, Raymond, for you are truly God's messenger.'

'Enoch?' Raymond glanced over at Tim, who replied 'I heard him too.'

'The Painting, you must burn it. Right now, on the grave, let its ashes rest upon the fresh soil. Do it now for we have little time.'

'Lighter?'

Tim shook his head.

'Inside the church, wait.'

Raymond rushed into the church, breaking police tape that had cordoned off the fire-damaged area. Candles were around, that meant matches, somewhere, but where? Raymond began to panic. 'Come on, matches, matches, where....there.'

Raymond broke into a small cupboard that had usual health and safety signs on it. It was obviously used for storing cleaning kits, chemicals, bucket. Matches.

'Got some matches,' he panted. 'Enoch, we are ready.'

'My son, you must read from the book.'

Raymond and Tim went cold. It was the feeling of complete failure.

'I just don't believe this – the damn book,' Raymond said dejectedly.

Tim Farley shook his head. 'I'm out of ideas.'

'And we're out of time.'

Enoch re-entered their minds. 'Bringing the painting to the grave has caused a paradoxical anomaly, it is creating energy that will soon open a portal to where we are. Raymond, I can read your thoughts, and you are wise. Between us, our combined strength and pure good energy will allow our Father to create a temporal shift.'

'It's Tim Farley, can you hear me?'

'Yes, Mr Farley. But you need not be concerned, as I

181

am aware of your next question. We can create a shift along the timeline within the space-time continuum, but only if Raymond reads from the book. You must read ahead. Blank pages will materialise into words. There will be pain and hardship, but he will succeed. Only with the books can we all be together again. Hurry.'

'But Enoch,' cried Raymond. 'We can't get the book.'

There was no reply for nearly a minute.

'Enoch?'

'My Son, you shall remain here. Mr Farley, you shall retrieve the book from the police car.'

'Police car, what pol...' He stopped. At the small gravel car park was a Ford patrol unit. A door opened. Out stepped the Chief Inspector from HQ.

'Damn it,' Farley whined. 'I don't believe this.'

'*Mr Farley.*' The voice inside his head seemed to echo. '*You must believe. Say it now. You DO believe.*'

'I believe.'

'*Mr Farley, time is nearly upon us.*'

Tim suddenly felt confident. This Priest from Rome was very special, he really did believe in him. 'I believe,' he said with pure glowing confidence.

'Hello Tim.' The Chief smiled.

'How did you track us down?'

'C'mon. You think I didn't know? That crazy scheme to break out, ditching a car with a tracker installed, and then arrive at a crime scene, with detectives in plain sight? I wanted to know what you knew, and whether that cock-and-bull story was worth pursuing. So I had the desk staff turn a blind eye, allowing your escape.'

Tim grinned and shook his head slightly. 'Of course.'

'Had some weird visions, like a voice in my head.

182

Thought, "you know, Tim's right". Went by the house on the way, picked up this book. Still no idea what's going on but I know it isn't voodoo. Here...'

Tim took the book and thanked him, and then thanked Enoch again.

Raymond took the book out from the sealed clear plastic bag. He opened it and flicked through the pages to find the latest written word. It was page 183. The rest was blank. There was no future, yet.

'Enoch, what have I done wrong?'

Turn over if you please:

'..........do not despair for we are here........'

Enoch spoke through his mind. 'Raymond My child, read Isaiah's words. Read out in your most confident voice in **Enochian** – the language of the Angels, in **Prisca Latinitas Latin** and in **English**. Read out for all to hear. Know the words of our great prophet Isaiah. Five lines in each language.'

'Enoch we don't have time for this, please. Enoch, I don't know these verses. Can you read them for me?'

'Raymond.' Enoch's firm voice carried strength. 'This verse must be read from outside of this realm. They must be read through The Painting for all to hear. Raymond, are you not at a church? Haste, the end is nigh. I must go, they are coming for me. You must save us all. Now, set fire to the painting – it will burn.'

The young student squeezed his eyes shut, thinking in desperation.

'Raymond, I also heard him. We're at a church right?'

'Yes. Tim, you go get a Bible while I set light to this thing.'

Before a minute was up, Tim had returned, Bible in hand. 'Name?' he panted. 'Which book again?'

'Um......Isaiah.'

'It's a big book, where in Isaiah, which verse? It's gonna be like finding a needle in a big pile of needles.'

'I know, but although it must be read from the Bible, we can still look it up on our phones.'

'Wise thinking.' Tim turned to the Chief who was standing in a state of confusion and awe. 'Chief, use your phone. Look up passages from the Bible, in Isaiah

184

about fighting despair, or needing hope, no, raising the dead.'

'You've gotta be kidding.'

'Look, you had visions, yes? Take a look around us, what do you see? What's happened today?'

'All I see is a church, and...'

'I never thought I'd be doing this, I never go to church, let alone try to raise the dead,' Tim screamed. 'Do it man!'

'Tim, you're crazy. Raising the dead? That's some weird cultism,'

'Do it! You can fire me later.'

The Chief sighed '.. all right.'

Between them they found a passage, a powerful verse. They all found the same one.

'Twenty six nineteen, yeah?' Raymond agreed. 'we all got that?'

'Yes.'

'Me too.'

'Okay, here goes.'

'Stop!' Tim pointed at Raymond. 'I'm sure I heard something about language and Angels.'

'Oh no, you're right. Damn. The language of the Angels. What does that even mean? I don't know.'

'Why in God's name can't he just tell us properly without riddles and games?' Tim asked.

'He can't do it for us, using God's name. I think he is limited, through rules, protocol. I guess there are strict guidelines in...purgatory, or wherever he is now. Let's just do it.'

'Language of the Angels?' The chief asked, raising his eye brows.

'Raymond,' Tim's voice was calm. He smiled. 'I read from the Bible....'

'...And I read from the book. Yes. You're onto something. The book will guide us anyway, I'll just read what's written; be able to read the two languages that I don't know. You read the English parts, yeah?'

They began straight away;

"Through our mighty Angel Raphael......"

"Per nostrum magi Angelus, Raphael......"

"Ol micalzo, Raphael......"

"Your dead shall live; their bodies shall rise."

"Tuus mortuus fuerit vivet; quorum corpora resurgemus."

"Par teloah torzvl; dazi torzvl."

"Ye who dwell in the dust..."

"Vos qui habitatis in pulvere...'

"Periazodi faonts a coasga..."

"...awake and sing for joy."

"...expergiscimini et quia cantare gaudum."

"...torgu od oecrimi."

"It is their time. Time, time again!"

"Non est in tempore. Tempus, iterum!"

"Inoas cocasa olani!"

The men stood as still as the statues of the church. There seemed to be no breeze, no sound, an eeriness within the churchyard. Yet there was a presence. Something was there, somebody was there. The light started to fade again, as if the sun was setting, there were streaks of colour in the sky, a mixture of a rainbow and an aurora. Then an icy cold wind hit them hard. The men dared not move, they looked around continuously, wondering, waiting, fearing.

A sudden flash of bright light was followed, that lasted just a second or two. A massive crash of thunder shook the church and the men.

Then silence, calm, tranquillity.

Raymond turned to the other men. 'What was that?'

'Aren't you into all this stuff, you tell us.' Tim felt uneasy, nauseous. 'My head is spinning. You all right Chief?'

'Think so. Never seen anything like it. It was, um, sort of, Biblical.'

Raymond jolted, he smiled. Guys, look at your watches, the phones. Quick!' As he spoke he pointed to his watch and then grabbed his mobile phone.

Tim stared at the screen. 'Chief, what time is it?'

After some deliberation, the Chief spoke, 'My watch is stuck at 2 minutes past twelve. The phone says.....mmm, something's wrong with it. Two minutes past ten.

Raymond nodded. 'Same here, watch stopped. Phone says 10:02. Same date, same day. Two hours....earlier.'

'I've gotta pinch myself, are we saying that, hang on. Either our phones are wrong or we just went back in time two hours, or we've all gone crazy.'

Raymond took control. 'We have just a few minutes to fix this. Let's go.'

'Fix what? Where?'

'Chief Inspector, drive us to 5 Pines Avenue as fast as you can, I'll explain on the way.'

In the car, Raymond ran through his hypothesis. 'Enoch, with help, guided us through an ancient, rarely used ritual, something only the Angels use.

Enoch is the Angel Raphael and the prophet Enoch. He watches over mankind, helps us, heals people. He's known in every religion, he was sent to Abraham and Jesus. I know this 'cos he told me in all those flashing images I had. And in ancient history he battled the Fallen Angel Azazel. He's also charged with ridding the Earth of Morax, Child of Lilith and Vapula. Don't you get it? Those were the Angels, or bad Angels who have been using the painting and Dexter to get into our world again – using Human form.'

The two policemen were absorbing it and trying to believe it. They'd read bits from the Bible of course, but until now, had never thought they would be *In* the Bible. Tim spoke up, 'If what you say is true, or indeed *real* and we're not collectively dreaming this, then we are all part of this – stopping the demons, fallen Angels or whatever. We're writing history.'

'Not really,' Raymond replied. 'Cos if what I think is about to happen, *does* happen, then we will never have done any of this, everything that has happened in the last two hours will be gone, written over, time will carry on.'

'Wow.'

'We're here at the house.'

189

# Chapter Twenty Five

## Paradox

Raymond and the two policemen rushed down the footpath noting that there was no blue police tape.

They could hear no voices.

Raymond threw himself through the open doorway and fell over Jasper the dog who was standing absolutely still. He glanced up at Tim who was slowly talking and pointing;

'I...think you....need to see......' he coughed, '...this.'

Raymond hauled himself up. 'What the....'

Inside the living room were Stan, Lyn, Reuben and Melissa. And himself. Great he thought, but they were staring at themselves. Their *other* selves.

'There's two of us Raymond, um, what has happened, am I seeing double?'

Raymond felt the hairs stand up on his neck. He was looking at himself, another version of himself. 'That's me,' he said blatantly.

'Uh, yeah, I can see that,' Tim replied.

'There was a time shift but the original, um, family members, you and I, are still here and we have, well, copies, second, um, I have no idea.'

'Raymond, why are they not moving?'

Before answering, Raymond needed to think. He came to a conclusion. 'We haven't caught up with this actual timeline yet. Look, the clock says nine minutes past ten, I remember this moment; we had just moved in from the kitchen and talking about Melissa calling up Dexter through the book. Her mother was against the idea. This was *before* she collapsed, before the paramedics, and before you guys came.'

'Well that sounds great but I am pretty sure this is in my imagination,' announced the Chief.

'I assure you it's not.'

'But then, how do we know *anything* is real?'

Raymond nodded to the chief. 'We discussed this before, and I used to debate this all the time at uni. Chief, we are all just atoms and electricity. Every time we think, we simply use electrical signals, neurons. A dream seems real at the time. So yeah, I know where you're coming from, but this *IS* real. I know it. You know it.'

The clock moved, 10:10. Two hours in the future they had read in the language of the Angels, a rite to raise the dead. Raymond smiled inwardly, he thought of the illogical, paradoxical situation. *Two hours ago in the future, that was when it happened. Past tense in the future.*

The two timelines collided. Raymond watched his previous version who was in turn watching Melissa who was holding the book at page 139. 'Future Raymond' could remember that part clearly. He also knew what was to come next. He had to speak to the dog, to ensure continuity. 'Jasper,' he whispered, almost silently. 'Go upstairs to your bed.' Jasper glanced up at him, wagged his tail and scampered upstairs. Then there was the scream, he counted in his head, one, two....

*Melissa screamed.*

*Calmness followed. It was beautiful. She felt herself walking through cool water, waves lapping over her feet, footprints left behind were washed away by the*

191

*next swoosh of sea. A cool breeze flowed around her,*
*calming. Beautiful.*
*A man, an elderly man, stood on the beach.*
*'Are you Dexter?'*
*'Yes, Melissa, you are my saviour.'*

Raymond could remember every word, but why was
he still there? He glanced at Enoch who turned his head
towards the hallway. None of the others, including his
'previous self' could see them, yet Enoch smiled, and
winked.

A sudden flash and crash of thunder sent the *future*
versions of Raymond and Farley, along with Paula and
the Chief turning to dust, fading away, vanishing into
thin air.

†

Melissa saw a flicker of light. She saw Enoch, there
were other spirits, like Angels, but good Angels.
'Return with me, Dexter. We shall release you.'

There were no more visions. She closed the book
and glanced up.
Enoch heard screams, screams of agony; but they
were not originating in the house, or even in that
dimension.

'Enoch!' Melissa cried out. 'Are you all right?'

The screams stopped.

'Yes, my dear, I am fine. We all are.' He looked at
Raymond and nodded.

Raymond's mind consisted of jumbled thoughts and strange visions. He could not quite piece it together, yet he felt as if he had been somewhere else for the last couple of hours.

The police were not in the house. They hadn't been requested to continue the investigation thus had disappeared from the timeline.

Back in the Toyota, Tim Farley gazed into Paula's eyes. Why he felt sudden passion he didn't know, but something was saying *'ask her you idiot before it's too late.'*

Enoch knew that the timeline shift had caused a paradox when two versions of some of them had appeared. This shattered the original space-time, severing the portal to the demonic world of the fallen Angels, re-writing a new timeline. The Fallen Angels had not understood the paradox and could not find the way through, they had lost Dexter, lost everything. They had lost The Painting.

'Are the demons dead?' Raymond asked.

'One or two of them have been around for billions of years. It'll take more than that to rid us of them, and killing is not what we do here.'

# Epilogue

## The Beginning

'Woo, that was weird,' Lyn said, staring at Enoch.

'Just had déjà vu.'

'Me too,' said Reuben.

'Jasper!' Melissa threw her arms around the dog as he bounded downstairs and greeted her, tail wagging. 'Ooh, Jasper, you'such a good boy, yes you are.'

Raymond glanced across at Enoch, who was smiling. He could somehow hear Enoch's thoughts.

*'I, Archangel Raphael, watcher of Terra. This time has taught me more than an Angel could know. I am now learned, most wise. I thank you all, my dear friends. I will look over you, guide you, comfort you. You, are my purpose.'*

Raymond returned the smile.

'Enoch, did you say something?' Lyn asked, pulling an expression of intrigue.

'Yeah, I heard him too, Mum,' Reuben added.

Raymond turned to Melissa. 'Hey, I have a feeling we won't be seeing the demons, fallen Angels again.'

'How can you be so sure?'

'A wise Priest has done what was necessary. And you my girl have worked a miracle. Dexter is free.'

Melissa turned her head and looked at Enoch, her tired eyes showing gratitude. 'How?'

'Let's just say that I had a lot of help. We are all free

now.'

'Help?' Stan enquired.

'When Melissa spoke through the portal to Dexter, I was watching. Good Angels were there. With your hope and your faith, we fought the demons. They won't be bothering us any more.'

'Please,' Enoch gesticulated towards the book. 'May I finish this?'

'Yeah, of course.' Melissa handed him the book.

He studied the picture on the cover, then opened the book to page 196. There it was, all in print.

And so he read;

# The Second letter of Dexter Manning

*My Dear Friends.*

*I know that you would have not read this page before all others, as it would have had certain dire consequences of time paradox. But I do know that you are smart. You are the smartest people I have ever known, and you are most wise. I'm delighted to call you my friends.*

*I am in a good place now, I am happy.*

*Thank you.*

*Now, you go and live your lives in peace, never waste a single, precious day, for they are all important, each one guided by movement of time, tick-tock like the grandfather clock. For me, time is not here, it does not exist in this state of paradise. Your futures I am told, I have foreseen, but you must, and you alone, must follow your paths, of which there are many, often filled with happiness, joy, sadness and tragedy. But you* will prevail and within the paths of joy shall be two weddings and I will be waiting.

And then sometime, many years from now, you will certainly join me, join us, here, walking on the beach, cool water drifting over sand, beautiful birds singing chorus all day, and by night billions of stars of Angels watching over us, keeping us safe for all eternal bliss.

Thank you my most Dear Friends.

Fear not, we are always here by your side.

Dexter.

# Family Tree of Dexter Manning

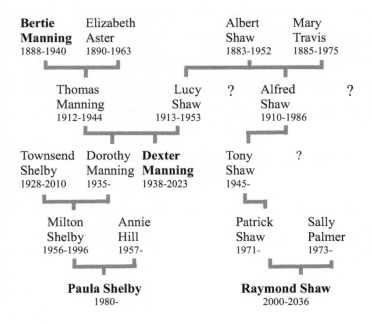

**Bertie Manning** 1888-1940 — Elizabeth Aster 1890-1963

Albert Shaw 1883-1952 — Mary Travis 1885-1975

Thomas Manning 1912-1944 — Lucy Shaw 1913-1953

? — Alfred Shaw 1910-1986 — ?

Townsend Shelby 1928-2010 — Dorothy Manning 1935- — **Dexter Manning** 1938-2023

Tony Shaw 1945- — ?

Milton Shelby 1956-1996 — Annie Hill 1957-

Patrick Shaw 1971- — Sally Palmer 1973-

**Paula Shelby** 1980-

**Raymond Shaw** 2000-2036

**Qui eripuit nos de tenebris**

**Resistere autem diabolo**


Do not look behind you for they have returned.


HE will disguise himself as an Angel of light. [2Co 11:14]

Now is the judgment of this world and it's rulers' cast out
[John 12:31]

And the whole world lies in the power of the evil one
[1John 5:19]

Lightning Source UK Ltd.
Milton Keynes UK
UKHW010930141021
392201UK00002B/301